Lady Isabella

Lady Isabella

EVERY ERA HAS ITS FALLEN
WOMEN

BY

Vicki Hopkins

PUBLISHED BY HOLLAND LEGACY PUBLISHING

Dedication

In honor of my great-grandmother, Jane Isabella Burrows (1865-1934). In her stubbornness she remained in England while her husband and children immigrated to Canada in 1910. She is buried in Southern Cemetery, Manchester, United Kingdom.

TABLE OF CONTENTS

ONE

SCANDALOUS BEHAVIOR

Butternut squash soup—the color, smell, and taste remind me of vomit. It's not the bisque's fault for my queasy stomach, although I would prefer to blame the cream base and the cook's incompetence. On the contrary, it's my fault. The reason for my ill health has become dreadfully clear.

Soon I will be the object of disgrace for our distinguished family. To be candid, there isn't a noble family in England that wishes to have its name identified with scandal. The connotation of immoral behavior, impropriety, or misconduct births malicious gossip that spreads like a disease, destroying social relationships. Those who can keep it a secret remain unscathed. Whether that will be the outcome that awaits my parents is yet to be determined.

Like most human beings, I put the fault partly on another person rather than shouldering the responsibility entirely myself. It all began when a new stable hand, Roger Gooding, had been hired. Perhaps I should blame Mr. Peters, our estate manager, for his poor choice in staff. Now that I have divided the liability between three individuals, it certainly diminishes my charge in the whole affair.

The moment I met Roger, I hurled away all reason. One could argue that most sixteen-year-old girls possess little if any common sense, which had certainly been my downfall. In my eyes, the young man glowed like a knight in shining armor in spite of his clothes that reeked of horsehair. His wavy brown locks and hazel eyes made my knees wobble. Frankly, I had never met another male that had such a profound impact upon my burgeoning womanhood.

Maybe I could have resisted the lure if I hadn't noticed the twinkle of interest in his eyes on our first encounter. I should have thought it cheeky of him even to dare to show me any regard. After all, I was the daughter of an earl and deserved respect as a proper young lady. At least up until that time, I could call myself decent. As hard as my father tried to instill in me the aristocratic pride of old, my small nose never lifted with any airs. With no blue-blooded ego to retain, I adoringly accepted the first wink Roger gave me, recalling how my cheeks burst into a blush.

After a few weeks of harmless flirtation, sparks started to flash. Every day that I saw him, my palms turned sweaty and my heart raced as if I had run the entire length of the estate toward the stables. When he made the first advance to disregard my rank in life, I became convinced that it was Adam who held out the apple to Eve. I distinctly remember the banter between us. Roger waited with reins in hand, along with my saddled mare. His words keep whirling around in my brain even today.

"You look rather cute today, Izzy," he said in a saucy fashion.

My mouth gaped open when he dared to call me by my nickname. Besides, I preferred Bella.

"Izzy? You're a rogue and much too familiar for my taste," I halfheartedly protested with puckered lips. "You just flatter young ladies like me so we will give you an encouraging smile in response." I found it impossible not to flash him a toothy grin, showing my pleasure at the compliment.

Roger nervously looked around, making certain no one heard his invitation. "Will you meet me here tonight?"

For a second my heart stopped beating, and my eyes grew wide with excitement. "Tonight? For heaven's sake, why would I do such a foolish thing, Mr. Gooding?" I reached out and patted the mare, appearing aloof.

"Because I want to steal a kiss, Izzy. Let me be your first," he taunted.

"Stop calling me Izzy." I hissed. "And what makes you think that a boy has never kissed me?" I protested. Naturally, I hadn't been kissed, except for an occasional sloppy lick from our golden retriever named George. My parents never let me within a hundred feet of another teenage male with raging hormones. He grinned at me like a fool. The idea of my first romantic interlude sent chills down my spine. Looking at his mouth, I swiftly relented.

"All right. I'll meet you here after dinner this evening." Hastily my mind raced through several scenarios of how I could escape the house unseen. "You may have one kiss, and that is all."

A suggestive smile lifted the corner of his mouth, but now that I recall the moment, his grin did have a slight wicked slant. Roger's eyes sparkled at the prospect, and I mounted my horse and retreated to trot across the landscape in a dreamlike state of mind. Had I remained another moment, I might have dragged him into the empty stall nearby and stolen my first peck on my initiative.

My downfall had begun as soon as I sneaked out of the estate unnoticed, clad in my baby-blue chiffon dress. I bounced to the stables as if I were on my way to the town assembly for a night of dancing. When I arrived, Roger grinned in approval. He gave me the once-over, roving his eyes from top to bottom. I noticed that he, too, had changed out of his overalls. He wore a clean pair of tan trousers and a partially buttoned white shirt that bared his upper chest.

"You do look beautiful," he said, approaching. Before I could answer, he slipped his right hand behind my neck, drew me toward him, and pushed his lips against mine. Astonished at the rapid onslaught, I could not protest.

"Well, good gracious," I responded, pulling away and gasping for breath. "You didn't even give me time to give you permission." I shoved one hand on my hip, showing displeasure.

"Did you enjoy it?" He smirked unapologetically. Once again, not giving me a chance to answer, his lips found mine. The next I realized, he had me stretched out on a stack of hay, feeling marvelous. His kisses sent electricity down my backbone. By that time, I had started my journey toward destruction.

After the magnificent joining of our lips, Roger discovered that I had never experienced arousal from a man. Surely, had my mother spoke to me about the so-called birds and the bees at a longer length,

I wouldn't have been so ignorant as to allow him to have his way with me. That reminds me that there are four responsible parties for my predicament. I might as well drag my mother into this mess.

One moment of unchecked lust had taken me to a pleasant, blissful state. Like a weak rabbit caught in a trap, I let him have his way with me. I assumed afterward he would propose marriage as soon as I turned eighteen and we would run away to live happily forever after.

If only I hadn't been such a simpleton.

How many times in life do we lament the "if only" acts in our lives? It should have ended at the first kiss. If it had, I might not be as terrified as I am now, looking into my cold soup.

To add to the injustice of it all, the next morning I found out that Roger upped and quit. My heart sank to the bottom of the haystack where I remembered his feigned words of love. He had lied and taken advantage of my witlessness, living up to the roguish term I had given him earlier in the day.

The smell from the bowl of bisque

continued to sicken my stomach, and I have concluded the worst possible consequence of my scandalous behavior.

"Isabella, you look peaked. Are you feeling all right?" My mother's voice called to me from across the dinner table, drawing me from my reminiscing state of mind.

"No, I have a stomachache," I answered with a sincere moan. My hand pushed the bowl of soup in the opposite direction. "Might I be excused?"

My eyes rose to my father, who naturally scowled in my direction and started his interrogation.

"Have you been eating too many chocolates between meals again?"

Chocolate. Visions of gooey sweets set off a violent upheaval. A second later, my hand covered my mouth, holding back the deluge. I sprang to my feet, toppled the chair behind me to the floor with a loud bang, and fled from the dining room down to the nearest toilet. As the vomit oozed between my fingers, I lowered my head into the bowl and expelled the balance of my stomach contents, which smelled like the tuna I had eaten for lunch.

"Oh, this is not good," I groaned with tears welling in my eyes. Another surge of my lunch that hadn't digested exited my mouth, leaving a nasty taste on my tongue. After the upheaval had ceased, I knew full well that I was doomed. I raised my eyes to see my mother standing in the doorway with a worried look on her face.

"I better send for the doctor," she announced. "You may have a case of the flu." Mother knelt down on one knee and placed her arm around my shoulder. "You should go straight to bed."

"Don't send for the doctor," I begged. "A little rest will do me well."

"Come now," she replied, picking me up into a standing position.

As I wobbled with her arm around me, gradually climbing the staircase, I wanted to blurt out the possibility for my condition. Mortified over the consequences of my confession, I repressed the urge.

"I'll ring for Hazel to get you out of these clothes and help you to bed." She pulled the cord that would send the ring to the servant's quarters. It only took a few minutes before Hazel appeared in the doorway.

"Yes, my lady?"

"My daughter is ill," Mother morosely announced. "Please help her out of her clothing and into a suitable nightgown. She needs rest."

Hazel glanced over at me. "Yes, my lady, she had a spell first thing this morning too."

The announcement sent a sharp pain through my abdomen. Why did she have to reveal that bit of information? I threw her an annoyed look.

"And you didn't tell me?" My mother frowned in displeasure.

"Miss Isabella asked me not to, my lady," Hazel said, defending her actions with respect. After a brief moment, she offered more damning tidbits. "It's been three or four days this week that she has awakened in a sickly state."

"I'm fine. Please stop fussing," I implored. Horrified over the news Hazel had blurted out, I cringed, folding my arms instinctively around my midriff. My mother turned her eyes to me and studied me for a minute. After she touched my forehead and discovered no fever, she suddenly changed her mind. Her eyes became dull, and I suspected she had come to a verdict.

"Never mind, Hazel. I'll handle this. You may go." After a hasty curtsy, Hazel retreated and closed the door behind her, leaving me to my judgment.

"Do you often get sick in the morning?" Her tone remained neutral.

"Yes, Mama. For the past week."

As she listened to my response, she ceased moving. "Have you... have you been late with your menses?"

I shook my head affirmatively but couldn't raise my eyes to meet hers. She breathed in a quick breath and held it, clutching my hands and squeezing them tightly.

"What have you done, Isabella?" Her voice rose, demanding an immediate response. "Have you been with a young man? Have you been seeing somebody on the sly during your afternoon rides in the country?"

Her grasp tightened to the point that I feared she would break every finger. When I tugged them away, she let go but seized my shoulders instead and gave me a good jolt.

"Tell me what you have done, Isabella."

After she had shaken me like a rag doll, I wailed my confession. "Oh, Mama, I laid with Roger Gooding, the stable hand. I didn't mean to; it just happened."

Mother halted her assault and brought both her hands to her mouth. "You laid with the stable boy?" she cried in a high-pitched wail.

I answered the question by nodding my head while warm tears flowed down my cheeks. Before I could reply further, her hand went up in the air and slapped me across my right cheek. The stinging force made me yelp in pain. Little did I understand that it was the beginning of years of bitterness and angry discourse between us that would follow.

"You stupid girl!" her voice boomed. "How could you be so bloody irresponsible to bring such shame upon us all? Your father. . . Well, your father will be livid. I dare say that I don't know what he will do." She peered at me in panic. "Is the young man still in our employ?"

My throat closed my airway, and I could scarcely choke out the answer. "No. . . No, he quit the day after." Mother's pale pallor had changed to beet red. My life had ended, and I knew it.

"Don't tell Father yet," I pleaded.

"I wouldn't think of it," she blurted. "First, we must have a doctor confirm your condition before arrangements are made."

"Arrangements?" I cried.

"Never you mind," she spat. "Now undress and get some sleep. First thing in the morning, we're traveling to London to see Dr. Richards."

As I watched Mother leave and bang the door on her way out, I imagined my life had ended at that moment. Briefly I considered jumping out of my two-story bedroom window to finish it all. The short distance would most likely break my leg, but perhaps I could lose the baby. Then, as if a lightning bolt had seared my heart, I realized the seriousness of my situation. The palm of my hand rested upon my abdomen and lingered there. For the first time, I considered the life growing in my womb. Overcome with emotion, I wept like a child.

TWO

PUNISHMENT WELL DESERVED

Lying on my back, with my legs spread apart, turned my face crimson red. My mother waited outside in the lobby. A nurse stood at the doctor's side. The cold white room and the hard table increased my apprehension. When he touched me, I nearly died of mortification. Finally, after a few minutes of the most humiliating moment of my life, it ended.

"You may sit up now," he said unsympathetically, pulling off his rubber gloves.

The nurse helped me from the awkward position, pulling the sheet up to cover my naked body. I sat shivering like a frightened and helpless animal.

"Have Mrs. Stuart come in," he asked the nurse.

I watched with tears moistening my eyes as the door opened and my mother entered. The nurse left, closing the door behind her. My hands gripped the sheet, and I wondered if they would use it to wrap my dead body. Surely my mother planned to strangle me in the next few minutes.

"Well?" Mother glared at the doctor.

"I can confirm that your daughter is no longer a virgin," Dr. Richards said, establishing my fallen state. "From my examination of the size of her uterus, as well as her symptoms, it is entirely possible that she is pregnant."

My mother's eyes narrowed in my direction, and I swore her hand twitched ready to strike another blow across my cheek.

"We won't know for sure until we take a urine sample," the doctor declared.

"Why?" I asked curiously. The notion of handing over my pee seemed nasty.

At first he glanced at me as if I should know why but then understood that my ignorance about these matters apparently had gotten me into this predicament in the first place.

"We inject a sample of your urine into a young female mouse. If you are pregnant, the mouse's ovaries will enlarge, confirming your condition."

"Oh dear," I whined. "Does it kill the mouse?"

"What does it matter if the mouse dies?" Mother shouted. Her voice reverberated off the barren walls.

"I just wondered," I sheepishly replied. Mother stormed from the room and slammed the door behind her. The physician appeared to remain neutral, keeping his mouth shut about our strained circumstances. He handed me a paper cup.

"You may use the toilet through that door. Please leave a sample on the counter. We will collect it after you leave."

I eyed the container for my waste with disgust and took it. "How long does it take for the mouse to do whatever the mouse does?"

"We will know within the week," he replied.

As instructed, I gave a sample of my urine that would subsequently be injected into a poor rodent to determine the outcome of my wicked behavior. The poor thing would be tortured at my expense.

However, as far as I had been concerned, my symptoms confirmed the dreadful diagnosis.

Since I knew exactly the time that I had succumbed to Roger's sexual prowess, the due date was easy to calculate. Late August of 1935 would be a date with destiny that I could not escape—unwed motherhood.

On our return home, Mother sat silently contemplating what to do next. As the motorcar drew near to the estate, she spoke.

"Let me handle this with your father," she casually remarked. "Arrangements will have to be made."

Arrangements. That word had risen in the conversation once more, and I could only surmise the meaning behind it. Would they attempt to put me through an illegal and dangerous medical procedure to rid me of the scandal growing in my womb?

"I don't wish to kill the baby," I hastily remarked, letting her know my wishes. Her head spun in my direction, glowering at me in half rage.

"I wouldn't suggest such a thing," she countered. "However, you won't be able to stay here and have the baby."

"Why not?"

"Preparations will need to be made to send you away until you give birth. Afterward, you must abandon the child for your sake and its." My mother expressed the words as an edict rather than a request.

Give up? My heart broke that it could never be mine. The connotation angered me to the core. The child was either a boy or girl—not it.

"Why would you make me do such a thing? Can I keep the baby and raise it as my own?"

Mother looked at me as if I had lost my mind. "You will not bring an illegitimate child into our household, Isabella. It's best for the baby and best for you." She looked at me as if I were daft. "You would be a child raising a child. It's out of the question."

"But—"

My mother raised her hand to halt the conversation. "Do you think that any man would dare to marry a daughter of an earl who has a child out of wedlock?"

She did have a point even though I hadn't accepted the fact that I had successfully turned myself into a ruined woman.

"I am not speaking about it anymore until your father has his say."

Instantly I envisioned him grabbing my curly locks and throwing me out of the house.

"I will do my best to protect you, Isabella. Nevertheless, the consequences of your actions will be a harsh lesson you will endure throughout your life."

At that moment, I learned that shame crushes your spirit, causing an awful pain in your chest as if your heart is being ripped out. My body trembled with hot tears pouring down my cheeks. A confession of contrition spilled from my blubbering lips.

"I'm sorry, Mama. So sorry," I wailed. "I had such a silly crush on Roger, and I thought he loved me."

The fact remained that he had used me like an irresponsible teenager incapable of control. Mother showed no affection toward me but regarded me coldly as if I had deserved what would shortly follow. Whatever the outcome, forgiveness would not come soon from the proud and socially correct woman who sat next to me.

After the car had arrived at the estate, Mother instructed me to return to my room and stay there until summoned. Eventually my father's wrath would engulf me like a raging, out-of-control fire.

For hours I paced to and fro in my bedchamber but heard nothing. Not even the bellowing voice of the patriarch of the Stuart dynasty, echoing throughout the halls. My mother visited an hour later and told me that I was to take dinner in my room that evening. I had no idea what tomorrow would bring and how it would permanently change my life.

At ten o'clock the following morning, the summons arrived to meet Father in his study. For the majority of my life, my father intimidated me at every turn. His heritage, rank, and property had always taken precedence in matters of family and relationships. Compared to my mother, who I likened to a cold fish, I compared Father to a rabid dog.

As I opened the door and entered, I instantly closed it behind me and approached. When I reached the distance of the two chairs in front of his large mahogany desk, I stood tall and brave. Underneath the facade, I trembled.

"You asked to see me, sir?" My eyes lowered to the red-and-gold carpet beneath my feet. I had never noticed the pattern before and suddenly became intrigued with the design.

"Sit down, Isabella."

The sharp command frightened me. Swiftly I obeyed, folding my hands in my lap. Mother stood behind my father's leather chair like a lifeless statue with no emotion. Not a glint of empathy radiated from her gray eyes.

"Your mother tells me that you have gone and gotten yourself pregnant," he began morosely.

Surprised that he didn't growl at me in absolute contempt, I finally lifted my glance to witness his down-turned countenance. My eyes welled with tears.

"I'm dreadfully sorry, Father, for disappointing you."

He cleared his voice. "It appears, Isabella, that your mother and I have failed you in some manner. I partially blame myself for my neglect and lack of interest in your daily affairs."

Blame. Did I hear Father correctly? Now I had five individuals to share the culpability for my wretched state of affairs. Speechless by his admission, I blew my nose into my hanky and waited for his pronouncement. He inhaled a sharp breath as if he needed it to restrain his anger.

"Regardless of your apology and my confession, we must deal with this matter expeditiously."

After nervously shifting in my chair, I swallowed the lump in my throat. At that point, I saw Mother turn around. Apparently, she didn't want me to see that she possibly had lost command of her sentiments.

"You must understand, Isabella, that I must protect the Stuart name from scandal. Therefore, I have arranged that you shall leave in two weeks for France."

"France?" I squeaked. My heart skipped a beat at the prospect of going to the Continent. Perhaps they were transporting me to a convent for punishment. I envisioned cruel nuns making me scrub dirty floors on my penitent knees. Within, I wailed at the announcement but kept silent as a remorseful daughter.

"You will be cloistered at a private residence outside of Lyon in the country. The parents of my solicitor reside there. They are retired and have generously agreed to house you until the baby is born. However, you will not be allowed to have visitors or be seen in public."

Suddenly my banishment sounded more like a holiday than hard labor, relaxing my tension.

"When you deliver the baby, you will not be allowed to see or hold it after birth. The child will be placed for adoption and given a good home. You will relinquish all parental rights." He hesitated and sternly asked, "Do you understand these terms, Isabella?"

My heart, bleeding at the thought of never knowing the child, ached within my chest. No other option or recourse remained. Submission to my parents' will had been my only choice.

"Yes, Father. Will I then be allowed to return home?"

My mother, who had regained her composure, answered the inquiry.

"No, Isabella. You shall not return home. We have decided it best to send you to Switzerland to attend finishing school."

"Finishing school?" I balked. "Switzerland?" I furthered my protest. "For how long?"

"As long as it takes for you to learn to become a lady," my father brusquely replied.

My mother spoke the final sentence. "No doubt you will not return home for a few years."

As my eyes darted between the two of them, they flooded with hot tears. Embarrassed over the reaction to my punishment, I covered my face with the palms of my hands and wept. A deadly silence filled my father's study as I blubbered my remorse. They remained silent, neither of them offering me a word of comfort or empathy.

"Is it understood then?" Father asked, breaking the silence.

My head nodded affirmatively.

"You will leave before you start to show

your shame to the staff and others. Nothing—absolutely nothing is to be spoken to anyone about your condition. As far as this household knows, you are being sent off to school."

Distressed and burdened, I begged my leave. "May I go now?"

"Yes," Mother answered. "I suggest you begin to think about the things you wish to pack for your journey."

If it hadn't been for some unseen force lifting me from the chair, I would have fainted. As I found strength in my legs, I turned and walked out, closing the door to the study behind me.

"I hate you, Roger Gooding! I hate you!" I bellowed sprinting up the staircase to my room. Truth be told, I despised myself for being such a naive girl.

THREE

PREPARATIONS FOR CHANGE

France and Switzerland. They both sounded continentally posh if there is such a thing in my condition. When my head continued to visit the toilet bowl, I wondered how long I would be in this state. The prospect of traveling such a long distance made me queasy. Mother indicated that she would accompany me on the journey, no doubt to make certain that I didn't get in any more trouble. After our arrival, she would return home leaving me in the care of a strange family.

As the weeks passed before our departure, I had started to feel somewhat better though struggled with fatigue. My thoughts frequently turned to the baby developing in my womb. As hard as I attempted not to become emotionally involved, I found it difficult not to love the child that I would never know. As I struggled with the myriad of emotions, sorrow seemed to be the one that overwhelmed me every day. Sorrow for my stupidity. Sorrow for my banishment. Sorrow for the baby I would give up.

My parents expected me to carry on as if nothing had gone amiss in the household, which apparently included dining with guests. The solicitor and his wife, whose parents would be my guardians for a time, had been invited to Kentwood. Mother instructed me to keep the conversation regarding my visit to a minimum, being careful not to give any clues to the footmen standing nearby. God forbid they should hear and carry the scandalous affair to the rest of the staff. Already I had surmised that Hazel had received a large bonus to keep her mouth shut regarding my morning sickness.

On the evening our guests were to arrive, I took particular attention dressing for dinner. I wanted to make a good impression regardless of my sinful state, but I knew that attempting to save face at this stage was a ridiculous ploy on my part.

As I stood in front of my closet deciding

what to wear, my eyes glanced at a red silk dress with a lace collar that I had purchased on a shopping spree but never wore. Mother disapproved of the color, so I left the tags on it and shoved it to the side of my wardrobe. Perhaps I should have known better to dare and wear it for the evening dinner, but since the guests were obviously aware of my fallen state what did it matter? I loved the silk fabric and dark red hue, so I removed the price tag from the garment and slipped into the luxurious fabric.

Afterward, my appealing reflection in the mirror stunned me. "*Elle est une femme éhonté.*" The French phrase drifted through my mind. "She's a shameless woman." Yes, and nothing could be done about it.

My hand glided down to my belly, reminding me of the miracle of life growing inside. Roger would never know that he would be a father. Frankly, I had not put it past him for having fathered a few children already. "Unspeakable rogue," I grumbled, casting the blame in his direction to appease my guilt.

With red lipstick, painted red nails, and a scarlet red dress that marked my situation in life, I descended the staircase and joined my parents and guests in the drawing room. When I came to the threshold, I pulled back my shoulders and glided into the room with confidence. Thankfully, I restrained my amusement at the reactions my attire produced. Father's mouth gaped open, Mother paled, and the guests looked flabbergasted. The hush lingered for several moments until I opened my mouth and spoke.

"Well, is anyone going to introduce me?"

Naturally, I glanced at Father since the dinner had been his idea. He quickly cleared his throat and shot an apologetic glance at the guests. The gentleman who stood near his wife appeared to stifle his amusement as if he understood my maneuver. Instantly I sensed camaraderie and smirked at him in return. On the other hand, his wife clung to his arm wide-eyed and looking offended. Glancing at Father to get on with the introductions, he finally spoke.

"Mr. Reginald Spencer and his wife, Catrina." Father paused. "May I introduce you to my daughter, Isabella Jane?"

Slightly stunned he spoke the name Jane, I had no idea why he included my middle name in the introduction. Confident and unembarrassed over my choice of clothing, I nodded and smiled warmly.

"It is indeed a pleasure to make your acquaintance."

"It is ours as well," Mr. Spencer replied still sporting that sly knowing smile. The gentleman towered over his wife, and I estimated his height to be at least six foot if not more. His wife appeared timid and quite short, no more than five feet tall. Her head barely reached his shoulder. I thought them an odd match for one another, but who I was to make any judgments above love and marriage? After all, I was the ignorant and scandalous daughter standing before them without an ounce of common sense.

"I see everyone is enjoying a drink before dinner, but alas I am still underage, and Father refuses to let me have a taste of champagne." Father flashed me a disgruntled look.

The awkward scene quickly ended

when the butler announced dinner. My parents led the way, followed by the Spencers, and I trailed behind them as if I were the family pet.

After we had sat at the table, the aroma of the first course wafted toward my nose. I thanked the good Lord above, who I hoped hadn't written me off as a hell-bound sinner, that my stomach had settled and I could eat. Being famished, I wondered if I would eventually crave odd food like ice cream and pickles.

Father and Mother entered into an idle chitchat with our guests, and I sat quietly observing between sips of my bisque. My mother's eyes wandered over to me and gave me that look to sit up straight and not slouch. I complied with her request. It had been some time since I had been invited to the dining table with guests. Children weren't allowed at formal dinner parties in our household. Since I was the only child, I often got shooed away and watched over by my nanny while they entertained. Tired of being left out of the conversation, I finally spoke.

"Mr. Spencer, if you don't mind, could

you please describe for me where I will be housed before I start finishing school?" I glanced over at the staff, hoping he got the drift not to mention the obvious. Not appearing surprised at my abrupt inquiry, he dabbed his lips with his napkin and gave me his undivided attention.

"My pleasure, Lady Isabella," he replied. "They have a modest chateau on the outskirts of Lyon. It's quite pleasant there, and I'm sure you will enjoy your visit."

"Are your parents French?"

"No, they are English but retired there some years ago."

"Oh, I see," I said, thinking that I would be housed with a dull elderly couple. They probably have nothing to do, and I would be their entertainment. Frankly, the entire arrangement appeared suspiciously odd. I hadn't asked Father how he came to this plan. Perhaps he sought legal counsel, and Mr. Spencer offered his parents up for the task. Unfortunately, I had been told by my mother not to ask questions and accept everything at face value.

"Do you speak French?"

Catrina interrupted my thoughts, and I

looked at her with surprise.

"Yes, of course, so language shall not be an issue, but if Mr. Spencer's parents are English, I probably will have no need to use it very often." They had probably received orders to keep me under lock and key until I gave birth but didn't articulate it aloud.

"I'm sure you will have a pleasant holiday," Mr. Spencer added.

Pleasant holiday? I nearly laughed but controlled myself.

"I will be traveling with Isabella to make sure she arrives safely," Mother declared. "The hospitality of your parents giving me lodging for a few nights is deeply appreciated."

"You will discover that they are warm and obliging. I'm sure it will be no trouble at all." Mr. Spencer glanced at me while Catrina remained quiet as a mouse sipping her soup.

"Well then," Father announced, "I'm glad that all is settled."

Perhaps for everyone else, but I doubted that I would feel settled for quite some time.

On the day that we departed, I gave my father a good-bye kiss on his cheek. He stood rigidly and did not embrace me with any affection. Guilt-ridden about my culpability in his obvious distress, I lowered my eyes.

"I am so very sorry for having brought shame upon our family." My voice cracked repentantly.

"Come along, Isabella," my mother ordered, tugging on my sleeve. "We have a train to catch."

Father remained quiet, standing in the foyer. He watched through the open door as Mother and I climbed into the car with our suitcases stacked on top and tied to the back. With one last glance, I lifted my eyes to our home that I would not see for many years. When I looked back at Father, he had retreated out of sight.

"He will never forgive me," I said, leaning back in the seat. "I don't blame him."

"Perhaps one day," Mother said, patting my hand in reassurance. "When you come home, all will be forgotten and you can start your life anew."

Forgotten.

I had much to forget! Especially the child growing in my belly. As I continued down the road of pregnancy, I began to bond with the miracle of conception, wrestling with the terrible grief that I would bear when my child would be taken from me. I understood why, and part of me understood the need that this must be the way of things. Nevertheless, it drove a sharp knife into my wounded heart.

FOUR

HIDDEN IN FRANCE

Occasionally in life, you have revelations about the motives behind your behavior and those of others. The trip from Kentwood to Lyon was long and tiring by boat and train. I experienced an eye-opening moment, during the extended journey alongside my mother. You would think that spending time together would have brought us closer. On the contrary, and I realized that my mother had always been incapable of forming close relationships with anyone. For the majority of the trip, she buried herself in a book and rarely spoke a word to me. When she raised a glance in my direction, I felt as if she were checking to make sure her extra luggage hadn't gotten lost.

As I reflected on her marriage with my father, I had to admit that they never displayed affection. Their life had been a coexistence of sorts between two people living under the same roof. Perhaps their marriage had been another parental arrangement. Obviously, I had been the only child born from the union, and I doubted there had been any medical reason behind it. Most of my early childhood I spent with a caregiver. To be frank, my mother had never been the mothering type nor would she ever display those qualities. When I pondered the situation, I realized that I had merely been a chore rather than a daughter, and it deeply grieved me. Her intermittent pats to calm my worries had been platitudes.

Finally it all made sense. Because of the lack of attention or affection from either parent, when Roger Gooding gave me the eye, I perked up like a wilted flower starved for devotion. No wonder I shivered with excitement and let him have his way with me while he watered my so-called drought. Someone noticed that I existed even if it had been for his roguish pleasure. Being able to make sense out of my actions had been a turning point. I understood why I had transgressed and discovered the ability to forgive myself in spite of it all.

Along with that insight came a self-made vow that I would never be like my mother. Even though she unsympathetically, along with my father, insisted that I give up this baby, I would never stop loving the new life imparted to me. In fact, my affections grew each day, and when alone, I would whisper words of love, assuring my child it had been wanted. I may never know him or her, but I would forever be a mother regardless of whether we were together.

When the trip ended, I found myself on the doorsteps of Mr. and Mrs. Spencer with Mother standing by my side. After the door had swung open to reveal my wards, a surprise awaited me. The elderly couple I had expected looked much younger. As soon as my eyes met their welcoming gazes, I experienced a profound sense of peace that everything would be all right. I wanted to turn to my mother and say, "You can go now."

"Welcome to our home," Mr. Spencer said. "You must be exhausted from your trip."

"Quite, I'm afraid," Mother groaned.

"Gerard, our butler, will see to your bags," his wife replied. "Here, let me take that from you," she offered, reaching out and taking my large handbag.

Gladly I gave it up and slipped my arms out of my coat, which Mr. Spencer grabbed.

"Let me help you with your wrap," he offered my mother.

She remained sullen in her manner, and her pickled face annoyed me. Instantly I assumed she was ashamed to be here alongside her hussy of a daughter.

"Please come into the parlor and relax." Mr. Spencer pointed in the direction of a large sitting room off to the right. "We have a pot of tea and cakes coming for refreshments."

"Thank you," I replied, seeking a comfortable chair. The quaint chateau was modest, boasting perhaps six bedrooms in all. The interior of the sitting room, expensively decorated with art deco modern furniture, was a switch from our nineteenth-century antiques my parents kept in our cold stone manor house.

"So your journey was long but uneventful?" Mr. Spencer inquired, sitting down on the divan next to his wife.

"Yes, nothing of significance," Mother blandly answered. She brushed a wrinkle from her skirt acting indifferent.

"I enjoyed people watching. There was such a variety of individuals traveling through France," I responded politely, acting far more pleasant than Mother.

Mrs. Spencer grinned. "Yes, there can be quite a menagerie of human life from different countries, including Germany. I understand the fascination."

Suddenly my mother spoke up with a rather surprising announcement. "I only need a bed for two nights as I will be leaving early on Thursday morning."

"Two nights?" I queried, swinging my head in her direction. "But I thought you would be here for a week."

"I'm afraid not," she answered sharply.

The glare in her eyes told me not to pressure her for an explanation. The Spencers glanced at each other clearly taken back by the news.

"Well, I'm sorry that you cannot stay

longer and take in the country air. It seems a shame that you must travel all that way and only have a two-day rest."

"It's my preference. I only agreed to accompany my daughter to make sure she arrived safely," Mother reiterated.

Her reply confirmed my earlier thoughts—her baggage had arrived in one piece.

"As you wish." Mr. Spencer glanced at me for a moment. "I assure you that your daughter will be well cared for during your absence."

The tea and cakes arrived, and my body, craving sweets, ate a mound of food, eagerly devouring the French pastries. My taste buds tingled with flavor after the first bite. An idle conversation ensued for several minutes between the Spencers and my mother while I downed the dainties. After satisfying my tummy, I yawned, feeling unusually fatigued.

"Oh, I beg your pardon," I apologetically announced with my hand over my mouth.

"Would you like to see your room, Isabella, and perhaps rest?" the kind voice of

Mrs. Spencer suggested, rising to her feet and extending her hand. The caring gesture of attention increased my respect. I needed a little lift to get my derriere off the chair, which I swore was swelling as much as my belly.

"That would be refreshing," I acknowledged, taking her hand. Turning to Mother, I invited her along. "Would you like to come, Mama, and see your room?"

She drank the rest of her tea and rose to her feet. "Yes, of course. A short nap would do me good as well."

Mrs. Spencer released my hand and led us to the staircase, which we climbed to the second floor. Ascending gave me a better glimpse of the chandelier that hung in the foyer. Each crystal sparkled like diamonds, capturing the rays of light from indoors and outside. The bright interior of the chateau lifted my spirits. We reached the landing and took a few steps down a corridor. My hostess opened the door and led me inside.

"This will be your room, Isabella, during your stay with us. I hope it's to your liking and that you will be comfortable. If there is anything that you need, please do not hesitate to ask."

My suitcases had been delivered and placed at the foot of my bed. After glancing around the spacious interior, I acted on an overwhelming urge and hugged Mrs. Spencer.

"Thank you so much," my voice cracked.

"Oh my." She giggled in bewilderment over my actions. "You are most welcome."

An anxious glance exchanged between my mother and our host, and Mrs. Spencer quickly ushered her down the hallway to another room.

I closed the door behind them and looked at the inviting bed beckoning me to plop on the soft silken bedspread bursting with a rose pattern. When I did, the fluffy mattress embraced me. A second later, I had kicked off my shoes, curled up on my side, pulling a throw over my shoulders from the foot of the bed. What a beautiful place to have my baby, I thought. A moment later, I drifted off to sleep.

FIVE

GOOD-BYES AND HELLOS

It only took a little while to adapt to the new surroundings, settling into what would be my residence for the next six months. When I thought about how far away I would be from England, not an ounce of homesickness ruined my attitude. For me, this affair would be a new beginning although it would not be without its inherent griefs that would ensue.

The following day, I spent wandering around the house and grounds. Mr. and Mrs. Spencer continued to be the perfect hosts. In their conversations with me, I felt no judgment over my fallen state but rather a sympathetic understanding.

On the eve before the morning of my mother's departure, she came to my room for a private chat. It had crossed my mind that she might leave and not speak a word to me, deciding instead to slip silently away.

Naturally, I was pleased that she had chosen to, at least, say good-bye.

"Though the trip was long, I am satisfied that I will be leaving you in good hands," she began.

"Yes, I feel quite safe here." My voice answered in a respectful tone. "Thank Father for making this arrangement. Do you know how it came about?"

"Frankly, that's none of your concern, young lady. Needless to say, he is kinder than I would have been had it been my choice."

Her unaffectionate words cut my heart. It had been foolish of me to think she would offer an ounce of mercy.

"Obviously, I have become a great embarrassment to you," I tersely replied. "I don't know how many more times I can apologize before you give me your blessing."

"Blessing?" she cried, cringing at the thought. "I'm ashamed to call you my daughter."

After hearing her punishing words, something snapped in my soul as I finally accepted the fact she didn't love me.

"You know what? I'm ashamed that you are my mother!" My festering wounds voiced angrily. "You have been nothing to me but a coldhearted stranger all my life who has shown little affection or regard." As my chest heaved in anger, her jaw set in defiance against me. "Frankly, I don't know if I'll ever come home."

"And what do you think you will do?" Her eyes cast a withering glare. "Find someone of your rank to marry you? You've ruined yourself and any possibility of a happy marriage." Mother took a step toward the door and placed her hand on the doorknob. "I told your father sending you to finishing school would be a waste of money. You will never be a lady worthy of respect."

After she had breathed her venomous words, I inhaled a deep breath for courage. I could not allow her to know how expertly she had degraded my self-worth.

"Then go," I entreated, my voice trembling. As my anger burned, she did as I ordered. The door opened and closed, and my mother left without a backward glance. At that moment, I knew that I hated her with every fiber of my being. While I stood staring at the closed door, I expected my tumult to well into tears, but it did not.

The next morning, Mother left early, taking a cab to the train station. She never returned to impart another good-bye. When I watched from the window of my bedroom the motorcar drive away, her abandonment broke my spirit. Not once did her head turn around to glance at where she had left her only child.

Despondent, I walked over to my bed and sat down on the edge, feeling numb inside. A soft knock came at the door.

"Come in."

Mrs. Spencer poked her head inside and looked at me sympathetically. "Is there anything that I can do for you?"

The gentle sound of her voice stirred my pent-up emotions, unleashing the floodgates of hurt I had kept locked inside. Sobbing uncontrollably, I blubbered my pain.

"My mother hates me," I cried. "I have made such a mess of my life."

No sooner had I expelled my sorrow than Mrs. Spencer gathered me up in her arms.

"Have a good cry, dearest," she said. "You've been through quite a lot, and you'll need your strength for what lies ahead."

I clung to her tightly, receiving warmth and understanding from a complete stranger.

"Give your mother time, Isabella. She will come around."

After a few moments, I pulled my hankie from my pocket and sniffled my tears into the cloth, attempting to control myself.

"You are very sweet, Mrs. Spencer."

"We all make mistakes in life," she began. Her hand brushed away a wet curl from my cheek. "It's how you grow and learn from your errors that will one day make you the woman you should be."

Grow. Yes, my entire body was growing, and my clothes were becoming tighter. I had no maternity outfits. Rather than deal with my emotional pain, my thoughts flitted to frivolous pursuits. Father had given me a small allowance for expenses.

"Yes, I am growing." I giggled, putting my hand upon my belly bump. "I'm afraid that I will need new clothes soon."

"Well, we can go shopping after your first visit to the physician. Your father has provided for you to see a doctor during your term."

At least Father cared about my health when Mother no doubt wished I would die. Of course, I could die in childbirth. The thought sent a tingle of fear through my body. A month ago, I wanted to die. Now I wanted to live to give birth. Clearly, I had become a jumble of twisted emotions.

"Come down for a cup of tea, and we can talk about what lies ahead for the months that you will be with us."

"All right," I acquiesced, hoping for more French pastries to enjoy. Mrs. Spencer had been more of a mother to me in the past ten minutes than mine had been in a lifetime.

After five months of pastries and gaining weight, the bump had turned into an enormous watermelon. Now in my eighth month, I couldn't imagine what another month of growth would do to my body. I already walked like a waddling duck.

My days at the Spencers had been filled with good company and small tasks to keep me busy. Mrs. Spencer, whose first name I learned to be Catherine, had become a dear friend. Mr. Spencer always treated me with consideration, conveying to me in albeit fatherly tones whenever he had something to say.

During the months that passed, my health remained good. A physician in Lyon kept a close watch on me, giving me assurance that all proceeded toward giving birth as it should. Delivery had been arranged to occur at the local medical facility.

As the time drew nearer, Mrs. Spencer warned me of what would transpire. In my heart, I knew that more good-byes were ahead. Good-bye to my baby, and good-bye to my refuge at the Spencers. Attending finishing school had not been my choice, but I knew that it would be a respite from life with my parents that I desperately needed. There would be time to heal my emotional wounds while attempting to turn myself into a lady of title as my father suggested. I refused to believe my mother's prophetic declaration that I had been doomed to a loveless existence. After all, what did she know of love?

I felt prepared for what lay ahead until my body went into labor pains. If the time had come to suffer for my transgression, God had rightfully given agony to women as penitence whether we be saint or sinner. The baby decided to burst from my body, and nothing could save me from that occasion.

Catherine sat by my side, holding my hand, dabbing sweat from my forehead. After all the months we had been together, I could not comprehend her kindness that never waned in spite of my failings. Had I been Catholic, I would have nominated her for sainthood.

On August 12, 1935, two months after my seventeenth birthday, I gave birth to a little girl. When she left my womb, I screamed bloody murder. As soon as she slipped into the world, the doctor cut the cord, and the nurse wrapped and carried her away.

"It's a baby girl," Catherine announced joyously.

"I want to hold her," I begged, stretching out my arms. The nurse ignored my plea while the doctor finished whatever doctors do after babies are born.

"I'm sorry, dearest," Catherine consoled. "It's for the best." She squeezed my hand in consolation.

The painful physical birth had ended only to be replaced with the tragic reality that I would never know my daughter nor would she know me. She wailed in the arms of another as she disappeared through the doorway. Perhaps she knew in her little heart that our ties had been permanently severed beyond the mere cutting of an umbilical cord.

Whatever provisions for her adoption had been made, I would never be told. I possessed no recourse but to agree since my parents forbade me to raise her. Nevertheless, I clung tenaciously to the hope that one day we would reunite. I secretly named her Mary Jane and whispered my good-byes through the hot tears of regret. Catherine heard my cries and hugged me in my sorrow.

SIX

POLISHED AND FINISHED

Father had successfully enrolled me in a posh finishing school near Lake Geneva as he stated. Apparently, having performed a stellar job in keeping my illegitimate child buried like any other scandal, the school officials had no inkling of my past. It was a lesson that good money could purchase anything in life, including my education as a lady.

With strict protocol regarding no men in our dormitory rooms and curfew by ten o'clock at night, I had no interest in involving my life with another man. After the ten-month course had ended, I received a summons in June of 1936 to return home to resume my place at Kentwood. Father had become eager to bring me back to England sooner than intended. Adolf Hitler had become führer of Germany, and too many political upheavals occurred elsewhere on the Continent. With memories of the Great War still in his mind, I understood his worry. Even I had become disturbed by the news on the radio. The entire affair scared the daylights out of me, and I was anxious to leave.

By now, I had been well taught in the skills of etiquette, civility, polite conversation, posture, poise, entertaining, social dance, and other skills that would eventually make me an intelligent and well-bred wife, albeit my morality had been a bit tarnished. Many other aristocratic ladies who came from families of wealth and noble standing attended my classes. I enjoyed the company of other young women my age and realized my gradual maturity into womanhood, having recently turned eighteen. I attributed the transformation to not only the school but also the fact that I had become a mother.

As I stood gazing into my open suitcase, my hands fingered the gold locket around my neck. Catherine, as a thoughtful parting gift before coming to Geneva, had given the jewelry to me. She had somehow or other managed to clip a strand from my daughter's hair and tucked it away in the center of the trinket piece. Her kind gesture had allowed me to keep the child that I would never know, forever near my heart, at the end of a gold chain. Every day I wore it and refused to take it off.

"Isabella, here is your sweater that I borrowed." A voice from the door to my room brought my attention back to the packing at hand.

"Oh, thank you, Susan. I nearly forgot about it. You are kind to return the item."

"Thank you for letting me borrow it." She smiled in response.

Susan had become a friend during my stay at Château Mont-Choisi. Though she never knew the meaning of the locket that hung around my neck, I trusted her like a sister.

"I will miss you." My hands received the sweater, and I looked at it for a moment. "Why don't you keep it? This old suitcase is bursting at the seams already." I held it out to her.

"Really?"

"Yes, please keep it."

"It's such a beautiful blue, and I've

always liked it." She took it and held it in her hands, grinning at the gift. "You have been a good friend," she added. Her arms flung around my neck, and we gave each other a tight hug.

"Stop it now, or I'll lose all the poise that I have learned and start to cry," I complained in jest.

"Write me," Susan implored.

"Of course I will. Your address is in my wallet, and as soon as I return, I promise to pen a letter."

With one last hug, I said farewell. My bags had been packed, and a taxi waited for me outside to take me to the train station. I felt no remorse leaving the school of etiquette, though I admitted the experience had been an interesting one, to say the least. Throughout my training, I learned skills but swore never to turn into my mother's emotionless exterior for the sake of propriety.

When I arrived at the train station with ticket safely stowed in my handbag, the station bustled with travelers. Frankly, I had forgotten the sea of human beings with luggage, rushing to and fro, with announcements blaring over the loudspeaker about departing and arriving trains on various tracks. At first I inwardly panicked as if thrown headfirst into a social world that I had managed to escape for some time.

Gathering as much poise as I could muster, I clumsily staggered with two suitcases to the schedule board to find what track I would be departing from in the next hour. Unable to remember what line I had booked, I halted for a moment, set my bags down on either side of me, and rifled through my purse. When I found the ticket, it snagged on my passport and landed on the floor. As I was about to bend down and pick it up, a pair of booted feet approached and a leather-gloved hand snatched it instead.

"Let me help," the male voice said. I lifted my eyes, surprised to see a military uniform. Mercifully, the armband showed no swastika. I imagined the handsome young man to be French.

"Thank you," I said, smiling. I stuffed it back in my purse, grabbed my suitcases, and shuffled away as fast as I could, looking for another schedule board.

Eventually I found the departing track number and headed in its direction. My anxious nerves had multiplied tenfold as I bumped into numerous people scurrying alongside railcars. The smell of iron, steam, and oil filled my nostrils. When I found the numbered coach, a kind porter helped me with my luggage and led me to my private sleeping quarters. Grateful for my father's generous allowance to purchase a first-class ticket, I tipped the porter for bringing my bags and slid the door closed for privacy.

Exhausted, I slumped onto the cushioned seat. Outside, passengers thronged the walkway between trains. Steam hissed from nearby engines. Watching the commotion left me in a tizzy, so I drew the shade and exhaled a sigh of relief. My poor hatpin had slipped, causing my headpiece to cling lopsided to my head. I removed it and set it down next to me. As I kicked off my shoes because of my aching feet, I examined my surroundings. They looked comfortable and clean for the journey home.

The travel from Geneva to Calais would

take nearly twelve hours, and as I glanced at my watch, I cringed that my arrival in Calais would be in the dead of night. I hadn't thought of spending the evening there before taking a ferry across to Dover and then another train to London. When I traveled with my mother, pregnant, I must have been in a daze the entire way. The trip home felt as if it would take an eternity before I set foot again at Kentwood Manor.

The whistle screeched, and the train lurched forward, beginning its smooth transition down the track. I pulled up the shade and watched as we left the station, saying farewell to the fascinating city. On our way, we would travel through Lyon, which only brought a pang of sadness as I remember the baby that I had given birth to nearly a year ago. Naturally, I wondered where she lived, thinking someone from the Continent may have taken her. It could even be possible that she resided somewhere else in the world like the United States. Thinking of her whereabouts reminded me of the gnawing void in my heart until tears welled in my eyes. I would never know, and it was fruitless to speculate about my daughter's whereabouts. Nevertheless, I prayed she would be safe and well.

Tired at the thought, I leaned back and then down on my side, bringing my feet up. I wanted to sleep the entire way but knew full well that my stomach would growl in a few hours, demanding food. Just as I felt my eyelids flutter to dreamland, a knock upon my door aroused me.

"Ticket, please," came the booming voice of a conductor.

"Just a minute," I called out, grabbing my purse and rifling through the contents once more. Retrieving it, I tiptoed in my silk hose to the door too lazy to put my shoes back on. As I slid it open, a tall uniformed man grabbed it, gave it a quick perusal, punched a hole in the form, then handed it back.

"Thank you," he said, walking down to the next compartment. Afterward, I slid the door shut, resumed my position, and took advantage of the moment alone.

After a deep sleep, I woke up disoriented two hours later. The train continued toward our destination. I stuck my head out of the cabin to see if I could find a porter. Luckily, one headed toward me down the narrow aisle.

"Where are we?" I asked, glancing out the window, looking for anything familiar. We were traveling through the country.

"East of Lyon," he said. He tipped his hat and continued on his way.

Lyon? I couldn't believe that I had missed seeing the city, but perhaps it had been for my benefit. I slid the door closed, and my stomach growled. When I lifted my sleeve and looked at my watch, it had turned six o'clock. The dining car would be open, and I felt famished.

It took almost a half hour to wash my face, change my wrinkled dress, and rearrange my curls that were in disarray. When I felt presentable, I finally put my shoes back on. They had a short two-inch heel but had not been the most comfortable as I had discovered, hauling suitcases around the train station.

As soon as I stepped out into the hallway, the train turned toward the right, curving around a bend. My footing, already unsure, caused me to bump into the window. I had forgotten the challenges of walking down corridors and between cars. Another porter came scurrying down the hallway.

"Is the dining car to my right or left?" I asked, glancing both ways unsure.

"To your left, ma'am, next car," he said, squeezing by me going in the opposite direction.

Straightening my shoulders like a finished woman should, I headed down the corridor. After I had reached the end of the car, I pulled the heavy door and considered the path ahead of me. Walking between railcars scared the daylights out of me. You could see the ground flying by between the cracks, and the clickety-clack of the metal wheels on the rails roared in my ears. All that stood between certain death and me was a flimsy metal strip, wobbling back and forth, which made a path toward another door that led to the dining car.

"You can make it across in one wide stride," said a male voice, coming up behind me. I swung my head around, thinking an impatient porter wanted me to get on with it. Instead, I saw a familiar face that I couldn't place. As I gawked at him curiously, he spoke once more.

"Allow me to go ahead, and I'll reach out my hand and give you a tug across the abyss." He chuckled.

"Oh, sure, with one stride I'm sure any man with long legs can make it." I balked. "With these heels, it will take me two to three nightmarish steps."

He smirked, pushed by me, and with one giant stride, crossed over and stood in front of the other door.

"Come on now. Give me your hand," he ordered, reaching out toward me.

Naturally, I glanced at the large palm on the other side and then lowered my head, considering the ground whizzing underneath my feet. My stomach growled again, reminding me that I could either cross or starve.

"All right then," I said, clasping my fingers around his warm flesh.

"One, two, three," he said. On three, I threw my right leg in front of me and went airborne. Thankfully, he pulled me toward him with a sharp jerk, and I landed on two feet.

"See, that wasn't so bad." He glanced

down into my eyes as my breasts pressed against his upper body. After he had cleared his throat, aware of the awkward position, he held my hand and swung open the dining car door. When he pulled me through to the other side, I suddenly remembered the gentleman's name.

"Are you Mr. Spencer? Reginald Spencer?"

"Ah, you remembered. And you are Lady Isabella Stuart."

Embarrassed that he knew of my indiscretions, I sheepishly looked elsewhere. Would I carry this embarrassment for the remainder of my life?

"Do you mind if I join you for dinner?" he asked.

Dinner? I had hoped for time alone, but it seemed fate had other plans.

SEVEN

DINNER FOR TWO

The dinner hour had just begun, so we didn't need to wait for a table. Because of my past indiscretions, I wondered if Mr. Spencer expected a silly girl to keep him company. Things had changed, and so had I. As my father hoped, I felt more like a lady, finished and polished from my recent experiences.

As we settled into our chairs and were handed a menu, I glanced out the window at the passing scenery. Dusk had painted the skyline pink. A few moments later, I turned my attention back to Mr. Spencer. His eyes perused the menu.

"I'm surprised to see you here," I began. Interrupting his focus, Mr. Spencer lifted his gaze toward me.

"Yes, I am returning from visiting my parents in Lyon," he replied.

"Oh, how are they?" I asked enthusiastically. "I dare say my time with them was most enjoyable. They were kind and supportive."

"Both are well, thank you." He hesitated for a moment and then laid the menu down on the table. "I'm attempting to convince them to return to England," he admitted with a worried glint in his eyes.

"Are you as worried as everyone else about. . ." I glanced around before speaking the man's name in a whisper. "Hitler?"

He shook his head affirmatively. Speculation of possible invasions by Germany of neighboring countries swirled. Many believed, however, that France could hold their borders should Hitler attempt to do the unthinkable.

"I hope they took your advice," I responded in concern.

"I'm afraid not. Father can be a bit stubborn though I think Mother may eventually convince him."

"Did your father serve in the Great War?"

"Yes, in France. He lost a brother, but thankfully he returned home."

"Sad indeed," I replied, wincing at the thought. "My mother lost a cousin in

Belgium."

We both fell silent, and then it suddenly dawned on me that Catrina wasn't present. "Is your wife not dining with you this evening?" My innocent question caused distress in his eyes, and he instantly broke our gaze by looking down at the tabletop.

"My wife passed away last year," he announced grimly. "It was quite sudden. An aneurysm in her brain the doctors tell me."

I brought my hand to my mouth, suppressing a gasp at the shocking news. "Oh dear Lord, I am so very sorry, Mr. Spencer. My sincerest condolences." My heart broke for the poor man.

"Thank you." He continued to avert a direct gaze, fiddling with the menu.

What a dreadful thing for a man to endure. Probably only in his early thirties and he suddenly becomes a widower. Afraid to focus on such sadness, I kept silent not wanting to pry further. Thankfully, our waiter approached.

"May I get you anything to drink before taking your order?"

"Do you drink wine?" he asked.

"Not usually," I replied. "Tea for me, if

you please."

"Coffee," he ordered.

"No, please, if you wish a glass of wine, do not hesitate on my account," I assured him.

"Well, if you don't mind."

"No, of course not."

"I'll have a glass of Chardonnay," he requested.

The waiter left, and I picked up my menu again. "Well, I better decide what to eat." When the server returned, I ordered baked chicken, and Mr. Spencer chose fish. As we drank our wine and tea, I considered what polite conversation I should raise.

"So tell me," he began first, "did you enjoy your stay in Geneva this past year?"

Thinking back when we first met, I replied with a straight face. "As a matter of fact, yes, but I decided to forgo wearing any red dresses."

A soft chuckle left his throat. His regard contained no condemnation. In fact, being in his presence felt relaxing—much like being with his parents.

"Your mother was most kind to me, Mr. Spencer." My hand reached up and felt my locket, wondering if he knew what it contained. "As challenging as the experience had been personally, their unwavering support and care for me helped immensely."

"Mother is the most compassionate soul I know," he admitted. "It's been difficult since the death of Catrina with my family in London and my parents in France. I prefer that they be nearby."

Family. His sentiment made me wonder if he had a child, but I refused to pursue the matter further.

"Are you looking forward to returning home?" he asked, leaning forward with interest.

At that moment, I looked at him more carefully, taking particular attention to his blue eyes and handsome features. A thin, neatly trimmed mustache, matching the color of his dark brown hair, added to his maturity. Still, a distinct sadness darkened his eyes. No doubt the death of his wife had left a painful scar, much like my own.

"Somewhat," I honestly replied half-heartedly.

"I would have thought you would be

pleased to return to life at Kentwood."

"As you know, I didn't leave on good terms with my parents. I don't think they care if I return or not." The thought of seeing my mother again instigated an ill-at-ease pull in my stomach as I dreaded facing her apathetic personality. She didn't even bother to write to me the entire time I had been away. Only the occasional letter from Father arrived with my allowance accompanied by a few pointless sentences.

"Well, I'm sure they will be happy to see you again."

Wanting to change the subject, I turned the conversation back in his direction. "Are you still a solicitor in London?"

"Yes, on holiday at the moment."

"Do you like what you do?"

"It's a job," he answered neutrally.

"At least you have a skill," I added. "As a young woman, I have no skill, except to be finished, primed, and educated how to be a proper wife and run a household. It's not exactly what I'd like to do in life." I wanted to add that my mother believed me to be unmarriageable material, so I might as well think of a career as a spinster.

"Is your father willing to send you to university?"

University. The thought didn't cross my mind. "Well, I've never asked, and he's never offered. I've always had the impression that he only wanted to marry me off." I grinned thinking of my grandfather. "You know, he comes from a generation where the education of women wasn't a high priority. My grandfather sent his sons to Oxford and married off the daughters."

Mr. Spencer considered my comment but balked at the idea. "Well, I think you can do anything you put your mind to," he encouraged.

"Perhaps," I answered, not actually believing in the possibility.

"Do you have a particular interest you'd like to pursue?"

The question caught me off guard. Frankly, I had never thought much about a career of any type. What did I want to do? My thoughts drifted to my daughter. Be a mother, I pondered inwardly.

"Literature. I would enjoy studying the classics and writing, perhaps." It sounded somewhat plausible as I offered the only inclination I could think of at the moment.

"You could be a teacher if you'd like," he said.

"A teacher?" As much as I hated to giggle in front of anyone, I couldn't help respond to his statement with a bit of hilarity. "Can you imagine my father, an earl, allowing his daughter to teach children?" I shook my head negatively. Unfortunately, I knew what awaited me when I returned home. It would be either Mother's continued reminder that I had turned into a useless and unwanted daughter, while Father in the meantime would attempt to wed me off and get me out of his care.

Our food arrived, and my empty stomach welcomed the moist, baked chicken, mashed potatoes, and greens. Not feeling like idle chitchat, I ate quietly but noticed that Mr. Spencer had fallen into a contemplating silence of his own.

"How's your fish, Mr. Spencer?" I asked, attempting to make polite conversation.

"Quite good. And your chicken?"

"Moist." We simultaneously lifted our eyes to each other and grinned.

"Call me Reggie," he said.

"Oh, dear, much too familiar." I recoiled. "I will agree, however, to call you Reginald."

"Oh dear God. Much too formal, Lady Isabella."

"Bella, I replied. You may forgo the lady."

"Much too familiar," he replied, smirking. "I will agree to call you Isabella."

We both laughed at our bantering. It felt comfortable to be around Reggie though I did prefer Reginald and decided so for future references mentally and verbally.

"Do people ever call you Izzy?"

My face contorted into its usual grimace upon hearing that name. "Please, no Izzy. I hate the name." His brow rose over my clipped reply.

"All right, Isabella. Point noted."

After we had finished dinner, he suggested we have a drink in the lounge car. Of course, the thought of crossing to another Pullman brought no joy.

"I will lead the way and help," he announced. "I'll even escort you back to your quarters if you'd like."

Remembering how he tugged me across and the fact that I landed pressed against his torso brought a slight concern over a repeat performance. As I recalled the moment of feeling the warmth of a male body next to mine, it had been the first in years. Of course, when I initially saw Mr. Spencer, I assumed him to be a married man. Now the situation had altered, which amplified my intrigue.

"All right," I replied.

He insisted on paying for my meal, and I politely accepted the offer. As I rose from my chair, like a gentleman he pulled it back, giving me room to move. The dining car had filled with patrons, and I followed him as he headed to the adjoining car. When we reached the door, he pulled it open, swiftly stepped across, and held out his hand.

"Nothing to be afraid of," he said. The assurance in his eyes told me that he would be a bit more careful on how I landed this time. I grasped his hand, and he gave me a slight secure tug, stepping to the side to give me enough room to avoid a repeat collision. However, he held me around my waist to keep me in a firm stance.

Once on the other side of the wobbly barrier, we chose two chairs by a large window.

"Please have a glass of wine with me," he pleaded.

"Well, I suppose that would be all right," I agreed. "I'm not much a wine connoisseur, so please choose for me." The fact of the matter at my young age I had barely tasted alcoholic spirits. Since he offered, I decided to relent.

He rose to his feet and walked to the bar, ordered two glasses, and returned handing me one. Thankfully, the carriages glided smoothly over the tracks. I attempted to position myself comfortably, crossing my legs like a lady and sitting up with poise. As soon as the alcohol touched my tongue, I feared red blotches would soon travel up my neck.

"If my cheeks turn rosy, it's just the alcohol," I casually warned.

"I'm sure your cheeks look quite adorable with a pink tint."

He took a taste of his wine and lounged back into the chair. The compliment took me off guard. As I pondered his choice of words, I wondered if he inferred he still thought me a child rather than a young woman.

We spent a few moments conversing about inconsequential subjects. His second glass of wine had replaced the sorrowful gaze in his eyes by one of male interest, causing my anxiety to rise tenfold. Perhaps he no longer considered me a child but an object of admiration, so I nudged the conversation to confirm my speculation.

"I enjoy being in your company," I sincerely stated with a coy glance. "What I admire the most is your gracious acceptance of my personality in spite of my past." My hand trembled slightly while holding my wineglass, having just brought up my illegitimate pregnancy. He appeared to notice and cast an empathetic look.

"We all make mistakes, Isabella. Even I have made poor choices while growing into manhood."

"Really?" My interest piqued, but he didn't elaborate.

"It's how we handle ourselves during the trials and learn from our blunders that define our personality."

Blunders. The word chosen pricked. I didn't consider my daughter a blunder but a gift in spite of my foolishness. Instinctively I brought my hand to my locket and fingered it with affection.

"Mother told me she gave you a gift," he said, looking at it curiously. "Might I ask if that is the jewelry piece?"

"Yes," I responded. My eyes lowered to my glass of wine. "It reminds me of my daughter, which by the way I don't consider a blunder."

Sounding offended by my terse reply, I took a sip of wine and glanced out the window. The sun had set, and suddenly I felt tired. My belly was full, and the wine had relaxed me. After his awkward statement, I felt compelled to return and rest for the next few hours.

"I didn't mean to infer that the result of your mistake in itself is a blunder, Isabella. Please, I beg your pardon. It's not my intent to make you ill at ease."

By the worried glint in his eyes, I sensed his remorse. Perhaps my tiredness had caused my grumpy response.

"I'm sorry," I said. "Frankly, I'm feeling

tired and should get some sleep." I glanced at my watch, noting the time. "How much longer until we reach Calais?"

Reginald took out his pocket watch, flipped the lid, and noted the time. "At least another six to seven hours, I'm afraid." He shoved the watch back in his vest pocket. "You do have a room reserved for the evening, don't you?" he asked with a concerned squint. "There are no ships to Dover until the morning."

A room? Good gracious. I fell into an instant panic. What had I been thinking? Reginald was quite right. The train would arrive well after midnight and empty us into a city that would be sound asleep. The thought passed through my mind earlier, and I had forgotten.

"Oh, my gracious," I gulped. "I'm afraid that I do not."

"Well, don't worry," he assured me. "I booked a room, and I'm sure they'll have something open when we arrive."

After heaving a sigh, I flashed a smile of relief. "May we travel together back to London?" The words flew out of my mouth before even thinking of the consequences of my question. Since I had been so empty-headed about traveling alone, I suddenly wanted the assurance that Reginald would see me safely to Kentwood.

"Yes, of course, I'd be delighted," he replied. He searched my anxious gaze. "I will escort you back to the estate."

"Thank you," I replied. "That puts me at ease."

We finished our drinks, and I set my glass down on a side table. "I should get some sleep."

"Let me walk you to your quarters," he remarked. Reginald rose to his feet and held out his hand. Without hesitation, I took it and smiled. As I felt the warmth and secure grasp of his palm, I regretted that I had suggested wanting to return. His eyes searched mind as if he, too, were hoping that I would change my mind. Unable to confess that I wanted to stay, I took the first step toward the car that led back to my sleeper. As before, he helped me across the joined railcars, and by the time that we arrived at my door, I realized that affectionate emotions had blossomed in my heart.

"Well, here we are," he said. "Safe and sound."

"Yes, safe and sound," I repeated. A warm smile spread across Reginald's face, and a look of interest flashed in his eyes.

"I admire you, Isabella," he admitted.

"Why?" His surprising confession startled me. Naturally, I thought it a bit ludicrous based on the circumstances of my past behavior.

"I just do." He paused. "It's difficult for me to express exactly why, except that I find you a fascinating woman."

Lowering my head, I fiddled with my purse, feeling embarrassed over his admiration. I had begun to wonder if Catherine had put in a good word for me during his visit to France.

"Well, I should get some rest," I replied, opening the door to my quarters.

"When we pull into the station at Calais, wait for me here so we can leave together." He put his hand on the side of my upper arm and stroked it softly as if he were reassuring me of his promise.

"All right then." Feeling awkward by his touch, I slipped into my cabin. "Good night,

Reginald." My hand slowly pulled the door closed between the two of us.

Somewhat astonished that a man had stirred my emotions for the first time since my girlish crush on Roger, I sat down and pondered my rapidly beating heart. No longer a foolish girl, I had become a young woman who could explore the realities of love. He interested me immensely in spite of our age difference, which I decided would deter me in exploring the possibilities.

EIGHT

NO ROOM AT THE INN

Exhausted but unable to sleep, I felt relieved when the train finally pulled into Calais. I blamed the click-clack of the wheels for my insomnia, but in all honesty, I couldn't keep my mind off Reginald. In a few minutes he would come to collect me. Gathering my things together, I slipped my arms into my coat, expecting the coastal night air to give me a chill. As I began to button my collar, a soft knock came at the door. Without hesitation, I slid it open to see Reginald standing there. A slight grin curled the corner of his lips, but he looked as exhausted and I did.

"Doesn't look like you got much sleep either," I remarked.

"You neither?"

I shook my head but didn't wish to let my gaze give away my reason. With both hands, I picked up my suitcases.

"Here, let me get one of those," he offered, grabbing it from me.

Without protesting, I followed him down the train corridor to the exit. As I expected, the cool night air met my flushed face. A porter offered a cart for our luggage, which Reginald took, piling my two suitcases and his on top. He seemed to know what direction to head, and he grabbed me by the elbow gently leading me forward through the crowds.

"There are always cabs waiting outside the station. We'll catch one to the hotel." A second later he yawned. "I'm exhausted and can't wait to get some sleep," he moaned.

"Me too." After dragging my feet to the cab, we loaded our luggage and departed. It didn't take more than a few minutes to arrive at our destination. I would have been lost if our paths had not crossed. Naturally, I felt grateful that in my absentmindedness at procuring lodging for the night, he would take care of my needs. When we reached the desk clerk and heard, "I'm sorry, but we are booked for the night," I didn't quite know how to react.

"Are you sure you have nothing?" he

asked. His voice carried a tone of frustration. "Are there other lodgings nearby?"

"I'm sorry, sir, but since this is a Saturday evening, hotels are usually filled this time of the night."

Reginald looked at me with a sad gaze. "It's probably a foolish task to attempt to find anything this late," he said. He glanced at the clerk. "Give me a minute."

After taking me by the hand and pulling me aside, I knew exactly what he was going to propose.

"Do you mind sharing a room? I'll sleep on the floor or couch or whatever, and you can have the bed."

Naturally, I worried about how it would appear to others, especially the clerk. I glanced over at him as he stood watching us. "Why don't you ask if they have a rollaway bed we can use? Most hotels do."

"Good idea," Reginald said, walking back to the counter. "We can share the room but were wondering if you had a rollaway bed we might borrow."

Since we apparently were not married, the clerk hesitated for a moment. Given the situation, I could only hope that we both would have a place to lay our head tonight even if it looked rather scandalous. I would probably never see him again, so what did it matter?

"Yes, we can accommodate that request," he said, turning the register around.

"Are you sure it's okay?" Reginald asked one more time as he picked up the pen.

Hesitating at the possible consequences, I leaned into him and whispered, "You won't tell my parents we had this arrangement, will you?"

"Of course not," he quickly countered. "I wouldn't think of putting your reputation in danger."

Even though he sounded sincere, I flashed a coy grin. "Well, it's a little late for anyone to save my reputation." Confident that he would treat me respectfully, I nodded my head affirmatively. Frankly, I was so tired that I could have curled up on the couch in the foyer and spent the night. Reginald signed the register, and the clerk gave him the key.

"Room 214, and I'll have one of the

bellboys bring the rollaway and bedding as soon as possible."

"Thank you," Reginald replied. He grabbed his suitcase and one of mine, and we headed for the staircase. My legs felt like wilted flowers underneath my body, and it took all my effort to climb the few steps to the second floor. Thankfully, the room wasn't too far down the hallway. After inserting the key, Reginald reached around the corner, finding a light switch, and flipped it on before we entered. Just as we did, I heard the rolling of wheels and caught a glimpse of the bellboy heading our way.

"Rollaway," he said, pushing by us through the open door. He set the small foldout springs and mattress against the wall. "An extra pillow and blanket are in the closet, as well as clean sheets," he said.

"I'm grateful for your help," Reginald said. He set the suitcases down, took out his wallet, and gave the young lad a tip. After he left and the door was closed, I glanced around our room. It was clean and comfortable, and the bed looked terribly inviting. It was big enough for two people, but of course that option was out of the question.

"Well then," he said. "I better figure out how to open this contraption."

"Let me help." After inspecting it for a moment, Reginald unlatched the mechanism that kept the foot and head folded against each other. When he took one end, I took the other, and we lowered it into place. The mattress looked a bit lumpy and old, and I felt sorry for him. The poor man looked exhausted, and he needed a good night's sleep too.

After opening the closet and finding the extra sheet, blanket, and pillow, I began making the bed for him.

"I can do that," he said, reaching out and grabbing the cover.

"That's a woman's job," I protested. "I'm happy to help. After all, I learned how to tuck a rather tight corner in my homemaking class."

"You did?" he said, watching me with a grin on his face.

I giggled. "Frankly, I don't think my mother has made a bed in the past twenty years, and to be honest, I've never made one either."

After finishing the masterpiece, I wasn't quite sure what to do next. We both stood there, looking at each. He didn't look embarrassed over the situation, but I felt awkward to be spending the night in the same room with a man. Perhaps I should have worried a little that he would take advantage of me and the situation, but in my heart, I knew he was not a scoundrel.

"I need to get my nightdress out of my suitcase." After picking one case up and placing it on the bed, I unlatched it and opened the contents.

"Well, we're going to have to do this delicately," Reginald announced. "Why don't I find my pajamas and change in the washroom."

"All right," I agreed. "You go first, and then I'll change afterward."

"Well, that's not right," he protested. "Ladies first."

"But then you'll see me in my nightgown." I scowled.

"Well, you'll see me in my pajamas," he countered with a silly grin.

The situation was becoming a choreographed pajama affair, and I just wanted to sleep. "Okay, you first," I proposed, "then when you come out, I'll turn around while you get into bed. Then I'll change, and when I'm ready, you can hide under the covers or something until I am settled." Thinking that I had solved the problem, he had one last question.

"Who will turn off the light?" His eyes sparkled mischievously.

"I will since I'm last in bed." I pointed toward the bath chamber. "Now go. I'm tired," I groaned.

After rummaging through his suitcase, he grabbed his things and retreated. He took his sweet time changing. I heard the toilet flush and the water running for a few moments. Finally he poked his head out the door.

"If you don't want to see a thirty-something-year-old man in striped pajamas, I suggest you turn your head."

Instead, I stood there like a fool and gawked at him as he walked in front of me. He neatly set his trousers, shirt, and other items down on a nearby chair. All of a sudden, I had a terrible curiosity flash through my mind about what he looked like naked. Apparently, I still had a tempting weakness in my personality.

"You looked," he said, pulling back the covers on the rollaway. He slipped in, lay on his side, but leaned on his elbow. "Your turn."

"Yes, my turn," I said, scurrying away. As soon as I closed the door behind me, I leaned against it and exhaled the breath that I had been holding. What in the world happened to me out there? I knew I could trust Reginald but was quite aware that I could never trust myself. Perhaps this had been a terrible decision to room together, but nothing could be done about it.

After the same routine of using the toilet, washing my face, and gathering up my clothes in my arm, I slowly opened the door and called out. "Turn around, please."

"Will do," he answered. The rollaway bed creaked as he rolled over. "It's safe now."

Slowly I tiptoed in my bare feet and put my clothes down on another nearby chair. The light switch by the door wasn't too far away, so I ran over, flipped it off, and turned back toward the bed. Before I made it safety, my toe caught the corner of the rollaway, ramming it straight into the metal leg.

"Bloody hell!" The words just flew out of my mouth before I could even think about what I said. I lifted my foot and hopped over to the bed. Of course the screech alarmed Reginald, who promptly jumped to his feet and flipped on the light. Tears rolled down my cheeks from the pain.

"Stubbed it, eh?" He walked over and stood in front of me.

"I'm sorry I swore," I blubbered. "But it hurts like the dickens."

"Let me take a look at it. Hopefully, you didn't break it."

"Break it?" The thought angered me. Just what I needed, a broken toe.

"Do you mind if I touch it?"

"Be gentle," I pleaded.

"Always," he replied, reaching out and taking my foot into his left palm. His fingers touched my reddened appendage. Gently he attempted to move it. "Does it hurt when I bend it a little?"

To my surprise, it didn't, but it was turning blue at the base. "Not too much," I responded. "Stupid toe."

"Well, it doesn't seem to be broken. It looks like you'll have a nasty bruise though." He thought for a moment. "I could ask room service to bring some ice. That might help."

Reginald continued to hold my foot in his hand. His empathetic gaze reminded me of his mother. The same calming and loving demeanor she portrayed evidently resided in his soul too. The trait became another endearment in the growing list of things that I liked about him.

"No, that's okay," I replied, slowly removing my foot from his hand. "I'm so tired; I just want to sleep."

"Well, if it starts to throb, let me know. I have some aspirin. You can take two to ease the pain."

"All right."

"Now get to bed young lady, and I'll tuck you in and turn off the light." He grinned.

"Tuck me in?" My eyes widened at him treating me like a child. I wanted him to see me as a woman. He waited for me to get under the covers, so I did. I almost thought he would bend down and give me a peck on my cheek and wish me good night. We exchanged a long silent gaze between each other, and I saw a spark of interest in his eyes again.

"Light," I said, pulling the covers under my chin and my gaze away from his handsome face.

"Good night, Isabella." He stepped over and flipped the switch. The room went dark, and I heard the squeak of the rollaway as he climbed on top.

"Good night, Reginald," I whispered. No other words were spoken between us, and a few minutes later we both drifted off to sleep.

The night had swiftly passed but not before making a fool out of myself in front of Reginald. Since the birth of my baby, I had been haunted by reoccurring dreams. In the early morning hours, another haunting scene caused me to whimper and thrash in my bed. The repetitive theme of a crying baby being taken away swirled in my mind. It always ended with my arms outstretched, hot tears, and a searing hole left in my chest.

When Reginald heard me cry aloud, I must have scared the daylights out of him.

As I held my face in my hands, weeping, I heard his bed creak as he rose and came to my side. Without asking, he sat down on the edge and gathered me in his arms. His comforting hands stroked my back.

"Bad dream, Isabella. Just a bad dream," he tenderly assured me.

Perhaps I should have resisted the touch of a male as I sat underneath the covers, but his arms of comfort enfolded me like a warm blanket. The pain in my chest eased, allowing me to take a deep breath again. After pulled gently away, the palm of my hands wiped my tears.

"Monsters in your dreams?" he asked.

I shook my head no. "Mary Jane," I sniveled. He looked at me cockeyed not understanding my explanation. "My daughter. I named my daughter Mary Jane." His breath hitched in his throat as if he were surprised at my response.

"You dream of her?"

"Of course I dream of her often but always with the same dream." My voice trembled replaying the act over in my mind.

"And what dream is that?"

His head tipped to the side as he waited for my answer, but I felt as if it were an invasion of my privacy. I barely knew the man, and speaking of my personal pain did not sit well with me.

"I'd rather not say." My eyes lowered to my lap, and I rolled my shoulder away in an attempt to convey that I wished the prying to end. My action expressed my wishes, and like a gentleman, he understood my needs. Afterward, he glanced at the clock on the nightstand.

"Well, it appears it's time to get up anyway," he said, rising to his feet. "Shall we go through the same routine dressing this morning?"

By the sullen look on his face, I concluded that I must have wounded him in some way by dismissing his inquiry. "Yes, that would work. Why don't you go first?" My words were firm, wishing to convey that I needed a moment alone. Without protest, he did so, and we readied ourselves for the day ahead.

NINE

HOMEWARD BOUND

We traveled across the channel to Dover on the ferry and boarded the train back to London. As we settled into our seats for the final leg of the trip, Reginald had grown quiet. In retrospect, I realized that I had caused his change in mood. Throughout our journey, I kept one lingering question firmly tucked inside. Even though I knew it to be prying on my part, I turned toward him.

"Do you have any children?" My stomach tightened anticipating his response. He slowly turned his head and gazed at me for some time before responding.

"Yes. I have one child, who was born before my wife passed away."

Reginald paused as if he struggled to continue. Anticipating more information, I felt slighted that he failed to elaborate. He gave no indication of the age or gender of the child nor who cared for him or her while he had been in France. After a few moments had passed, I noticed the former sadness in his eyes return. My inquiry perhaps had resurrected the sorrow of the passing of his wife, and I felt sorry for the child who lost a mother.

"I have something to ask you," he suddenly announced. He reached over and picked up my hand, holding it gently. His thumb rubbed across my flesh back and forth.

"All right, ask," I replied, wondering if he would bring up Mary Jane.

"Do you think. . ." He halted and gulped. "Do you think that we might see each other occasionally?"

Taken back by his suggestion, my mouth gaped open in surprise. Even though secretly I had hoped that would be the case, I couldn't believe he articulated the same desire. I liked Reginald—immensely. Despite our age difference, I felt drawn to him and his kindness.

"Might we clarify that inquiry?" Slyly grinning, I continued. "Are you asking to nurture our acquaintance as a friendship or do you have other objectives in mind?"

He stared at me for some time, and my eyes searched him for an indication. He blinked, then his gaze lowered to my lips. Before I could say another word, Reginald placed his mouth on mine. His touch was tender and his taste sweet. Naturally, I did not protest even when his hand came to the side of my face. He pulled back to observe my reaction and explained himself.

"I know," he said, "it was cheeky of me to kiss you without asking. Hopefully, that answers your question."

"Why?" It was the only word that I could think of at the moment. Why did he want to pursue me of all people? I still considered myself ruined and unworthy. "After what I've done?" I lowered my voice to a whisper. "By all accounts, I am a fallen woman with an illegitimate child."

"Well, the only thing that you have done as far as I'm concerned, Isabella, is to capture my fancy." His finger stroked the side of my cheek. "You have matured and grown into an intriguing young lady." His hand tightened its grip. "Forget the past and let us see what might be in the future."

Of course my parents drifted into my mind, spoiling the mood. They could vehemently disapprove of the dalliance. At least Father might, thinking that I deserved better in spite of myself. Mother would no doubt be surprised that anyone found an interest in me at all.

"I would think that I might be a conflict of interest should my father discover our relationship," I blurted in a worrisome tone.

"Ah, yes, your father. I hadn't thought about that," he said, leaning back in his seat and blowing out a puff of air.

"Well, we needn't speak of it early on." My heart thumped in my chest afraid that I had just sabotaged his proposition. "Perhaps we could see each other occasionally in secret and see how it progresses."

He shook his head and scowled. "On second thought, I don't think that your father would approve of a solicitor courting you, neither would my business partner."

Afraid that he would change his mind, I suddenly lunged in his direction, not caring who in the railcar witnessed my behavior. When my lips met his mouth, he put his arms around me and drew me closer, kissing me in return. Finally aware of my brash position, I pulled away and glanced at him with a sassy grin.

"Does that answer your question?" I posed.

"Absolutely."

"Then I shall be delighted to get to know you better, Reginald."

His hand brushed a stray curl that had fallen into my eyes during my whirl in his direction, and in his eyes I witnessed affection.

We held hands the remainder of the trip, chatting about trivial matters. All the while, my heart fluttered in my chest like an excited butterfly that a man had found interest in me in spite of myself.

Naturally, in the back of my mind, the looming objection from my parents cautioned me not to throw all my emotions into our arrangement at once. I wanted to get to know him and learn more about his child. What if we fell in love and eventually married? Would I then be a stepmother? Would that fill the terrible void in my heart?

As the train drew into the station, I felt a pang of sadness that soon we would part.

"When shall I see you again?" my voice inquired anxiously. I wanted to cling to the hope of our next encounter.

"I'm not sure," he responded. "You may telephone me after you're settled, and we can arrange a rendezvous." He pulled out a business card from his wallet. "Here is my office number. I've written my home telephone on the reverse side should you wish to call me."

After taking the card, I flipped it over and saw the penned numbers. "All right, after I'm settled and can find a private moment, I'll telephone." The train stopped as I put the card into my purse in a safe place.

We gathered our luggage, hailed a cab, and Reginald escorted me back to Kentwood as he promised. When the motorcar turned up the drive and I saw the house in the distance, anxiety choked my breath. Instead of feeling excited to be home, I felt dread, fearing the unknown. Reginald didn't notice until the car stopped, and he helped me out, holding my hand.

"Are you all right?" He shot me a worried glance.

"A bit apprehensive," I replied. The door swung open, and both my parents stepped outdoors at the same time.

"Reginald," my father said, walking toward him. "I'm surprised to see you here." Father shot an alarmed look in my direction.

"Yes, sir. As fate would have it, I happened to be in Lyon visiting my parents and boarded the same train on the return home. Lady Isabella and I crossed paths, and I promised to see her home securely."

"Well then, thank you for delivering her here safe and sound," Father replied.

"I will take my leave," Reginald announced. He set my suitcases down, and the footman scurried out and picked them up.

"Lady Isabella, it's been a pleasure," he politely announced, tipping his hat. He showed nothing more than respect in the presence of my parents.

Naturally, I dared not gush over the man but merely nodded my head in deference. "Thank you for your assistance."

Reginald climbed back into the cab, and I tried not to die a thousand deaths inside, watching him depart. Pulling my attention back to my parents, I flashed a weak grin.

"Father, Mother, it is good to see you." Mother took a step toward me and eyed me up and down.

"You look well," she said.

"I am well, thank you."

"Come in and have a cup of tea and relax from your long trip," Father suggested. "You can tell us about Switzerland and your schooling."

Yes, my education. He would judge me for the next few weeks to see if his money had been well spent. Undoubtedly, both of them hoped a lady had returned with intellect and good character. My stomach knotted, and I wished that Reginald would hold me in his arms and tell me all would be well.

As we entered the house, I glanced at my surroundings. Absolutely nothing had changed. The same décor greeted my return. Giles, our butler, smiled, showing his pleasure.

"Welcome home, Lady Isabella," he hailed, bowing his head. "If there is anything that you require, please let me know. We will see to it immediately."

"Thank you, Giles."

When I walked into the parlor, I chose a single winged chair to sit in rather than share a seat with either of my parents. My emotions for both had changed. My heart had turned stone cold toward my family.

"Tell me, Isabella," Father started, "how is the political climate in Europe?"

"Uneasy," I replied with one word. Not interested in giving a civil discourse, I brushed a wrinkle from my skirt in indifference. Mother handed me a cup of tea that she had poured.

"Yes, I imagine so," he replied. "Nevertheless, the season has begun, and I've brought you home to pursue other endeavors."

"Other endeavors?" I asked, raising a curious brow.

"Finding you a husband, of course," Mother interjected.

Irritated, I inhaled a breath before speaking my mind. "I'm here but five minutes and you wish to send me off again, I see."

"We only have your best interests at

heart," Father clarified.

"Well, you can be assured that your money was well spent upon my studies at finishing school," I added snidely. "Hopefully, you'll think me more of a lady rather than a trollop."

My parents exchanged a troublesome glance between one another. The next question flew out between my lips before I could stop myself.

"Do you know how my daughter is? Do you know where she's at and if she's well?"

Mother set her teacup down on the saucer with a loud clink. Father, on the other hand, narrowed his eyes.

"The welfare of your child is unknown. I suggest, Isabella, that you drop the subject entirely," Mother ordered. Her lips were pressed in a straight line, and the veins in her neck bulged with anger. Obviously, the subject was not to be spoken of in the household.

"I've spent time, money, and energy to keep your indiscretion quiet," Father said. "None of the staff knows, except Hazel, who is sworn to secrecy. Now that you have returned to this household, the subject it not to be spoken of again." He inhaled a fiery breath. "Do you understand me, young lady?"

Foolishly I thought that as grandparents they might have cared for the child I bore or at least knew of my daughter's welfare. Apparently, my assumptions were far from accurate. Neither of them cared. My baby girl had become an object of shame, to be forgotten and pushed aside as illegitimate and unworthy of the Stuart name. Instinctively my hand came to my locket and touched it reverently. I would die before I told my parents the contents of the only part of Mary Jane that I was able to keep. Eventually I acquiesced to Father's edict.

"Of course. Far be it from me to cause further scandal to this family." I rose to my feet. "Now if you'll excuse me, I'd like to return to my room and rest. The trip was tiring."

After setting my teacup down on the side table, I respectfully nodded to them both. Frankly, I didn't have the strength to smile at either of them. Instead, I left the parlor and slowly climbed the staircase to my room. When I opened the door, I noticed my suitcases at the foot of the bed. At first glance, nothing had changed. Oddly, though, the pink décor seemed quite childish to me now, and an overwhelming urge to redecorate the interior gave rise in my mind. Isabella Stuart had changed and matured. No longer was I the imprudent young girl who made a poor choice. No, I had grown, become a mother, and a determined young lady.

Sitting down at the edge of my bed, I pulled out the business card from my purse that Reginald had given me. For propriety's sake, I would wait a few days before telephoning. First I needed to settle in and get used to being back home.

TEN

A SECRET RENDEZVOUS

My parents had been quite busy arranging my life upon my return home to Kentwood. A variety of social events had been lined up for the months ahead. My coming out would never happen, of course, and no presentation to court would transpire. In all honesty, it would have been a farce, but somehow invitations to affairs arrived in spite of it all.

There were dinner parties, charity, and sporting events to fill my calendar. Mother acted keen to involve me in social activities to get noticed and married off. I, on the other hand, only wanted to see Reginald. To fit the part, Father gave me a generous allowance to shop for a new wardrobe. Unbeknownst to him, it would give me an excuse to leave Kentwood.

As the days passed, I impatiently waited for a moment to use the telephone unseen and unheard. Father had left the estate on business, and Mother had retired to bed due to a headache. I slipped into my father's study, holding the card Reginald had given me, and dialed the number. Since it had been a workweek, I phoned his office. After a few rings, someone answered the call. Instead of his voice, I heard that of a woman's.

"Beechen, Smith, and Spencer. How may I help you?"

After not hearing Reginald answer the telephone, I became tongue-tied.

"Hello, may I help you?"

"I would like to speak to Mr. Spencer if you please," I timidly squeaked.

"He's in a meeting. You may leave a message with your name and number, and I will be sure he receives it."

Afraid to do so, I stuttered my response. "N-no thank you." In a fit of frustration, I nearly dropped the receiver onto the base. Calling him at the office would not suffice. Somehow I would have to do so quietly in the evening but had no idea how to find the privacy.

Then I thought of calling his home number. Perhaps I could leave a message there. Anxious to let him know I had at least tried, I turned the card over and dialed again. The phone rang four times, and just as I was about to hang up, a voice answered.

"Mr. Spencer's residence." The friendly female voice sounded more welcoming than the professional one I had recently encountered at the firm.

"Is Mr. Spencer there?" I knew he wasn't, but I wanted to see what the woman would say.

"No, ma'am, he's at work. Can I take a message?" she asked with a cockney accent.

"Oh, well, just tell him that Bella called. I'm an old friend of the family," I replied.

"Do you want to leave your—?" Her words cut off when I heard a child scream in the background. "Hold on a minute." She gasped, putting the phone receiver down on a table with a clunk. In the background, I heard her calmly say, "Now what did you get yourself into?" A few moments later, she picked up the receiver again. "Sorry, miss, the little one took a tumble," she stated, out of breath.

"Are you the nanny?" I asked, not thinking it might be a rude and intrusive question.

"Yes, miss. Now, who did you say you were?"

"Bella," I replied. "Just tell him Bella called." I hesitated to say anything more except "good-bye" and hung up the telephone.

Well, that answered my question. He had a young child, but I still didn't know the gender. I should have asked but didn't have the sense to do so. Frustrated, I sat down in a chair across from my father's desk, wondering how in the world I would ever be able to contact Reginald, let alone spend time with him. There had to be an answer to this conundrum, but it wouldn't come today.

As I sat there pondering, suddenly the telephone rang, scaring the daylights out of me. After one ring, I grabbed it before the staff did.

"Hello."

"Isabella, is that you?"

Shocked that Reginald was at the other end, I nearly choked out my answer. "Yes, yes, it's me. I just tried to call."

"I know. My nanny telephoned me at

the office and said you'd left a message at the house."

"I called your office too, but you were in a meeting, so I hung up."

"Best not to call me here," he whispered. "Oddly enough, I had a meeting with your father. He just left, so I knew I'd have a few minutes to catch you before he came home."

"Oh, Reginald," I cooed like a schoolgirl. "I miss you."

"And I you," he speedily replied. "You have been on my mind since I brought you home. How are things?"

"All right, I suppose. My relationship with my parents remains strained, and they have plans to push me into social circles, hoping to marry me off."

Reginald chuckled. "I thought as much," he replied. "So when can I see you?"

"I will be in London on Thursday, shopping. Could we meet for lunch?"

"Not near my office," he said. "Someone might recognize us together."

"All right. Where then?"

"There is a pub in Soho. Would that do?"

"Yes, that would do nicely. What is the

address?" I grabbed a pen and notepad off my father's desk and scribbled down the name and location. "I do so look forward to seeing you again," I said.

"Until then, Isabella. I must go now." He cut me off, and I heard male voices in the background.

"Good-bye," I replied. He said nothing more and hung up the phone. Returning the notepad and pen to where I had found it on Father's desk, I went back to my room giddy with excitement.

When Thursday arrived, I called a cab to pick me up at our home, but my escape hadn't gone as planned without a confrontation with Mother.

"Where are you off to?" she said, accosting me by the front door.

"Shopping," I replied. "Don't you remember that I mentioned last night I'd be shopping today with the allowance that Father gave me?"

"Well, I should come with you," she firmly declared.

"No!" My voice echoed in the foyer. Mother jolted at my unladylike command.

"What are you up to, young lady?" Her eyes narrowed at me, and she took an intimidating step closer.

"Nothing," I said, softening my tone. "I would prefer to shop on my own. After all, I'm no longer a child." Mother cast a wary look in my direction.

"Fine," she relented. "Well, you might as well shop for a dress and hat. The Royal Ascot is next week, and Father wishes you to attend."

The Royal Ascot. I had never been, and a surge of excitement coursed through my veins. Being admitted to the Royal Enclosure was an honor, to say the least. Naturally, I wondered what their plans were for allowing me to attend such a high-society function.

"All right, I will keep that in mind," I replied.

She turned and walked away, thankfully without a further word. After she had disappeared, I exited the house to my waiting cab.

"Where to, miss?"

"Harrods."

Since I had a few hours before my

rendezvous, I thought that I would at least begin a shopping spree. If I came home empty-handed, it would raise suspicion.

When the taxi dropped me off, I entered the store headed straight for the women's dresses. As instructed, I should have shopped with the purpose of purchasing clothes for my upcoming social activities, but I only had Reginald in mind. I wondered what his preferences were in female clothing and remembered his shy wife who came to dinner years ago. She dressed conservatively that evening, matching her personality, while I, on the other hand, wore crimson red.

Deciding to choose the route of maturity to show Reginald that I was a woman and no longer a silly girl, I tried on a few dresses that attained that goal. When I found two that I liked, I paid the bill and hired another cab to take me to the pub. With bags in tow, I decided to search for a hat at a millinery store after lunch.

When I arrived and exited the cab, I examined the exterior of the establishment. Soho had not been an area of London that I frequented, so I doubted anyone who knew my family would recognize me in the area.

After pushing my way through the heavy wooden front door, I halted. It took my eyes a few moments to adjust because of the dark interior. My nose wrinkled at the smell of cigarette smoke and food aromas. When I finally made out the landscape of my surroundings, I glanced around and caught sight of Reginald, sitting at a table off to the left. He waved at me, and as soon as I started walking in his direction, he rose to his feet.

"Let me help you. It looks like you've been shopping," Reginald cheerfully greeted. He grabbed the two bags out of my hands and placed them on an empty chair at the table.

"Yes, dress shopping," I replied. He looked dreamy in a three-piece business suit. It was blue with gray pinstripes. His hair was slicked back and neat, and his trimmed mustache defined his smiling upper lip. As I glanced down at my plain day dress, I scolded myself for not choosing something a bit more fashionable for our meeting.

Reginald pulled out the chair and

helped me get settled and then sat across the table. He looked at me attentively, grinning from ear to ear. Naturally, I couldn't help but return his infectious fondness.

"You look beautiful," he said.

A burst of heat filled my cheeks, turning them red. Reginald chuckled as if he sensed my embarrassment by the compliment.

"You look dapper too," I added with a flirty gaze. "I like your suit."

The sensations of male enticement bubbled inside, reminding me of the danger of letting them run loose. As I regarded Reginald, though, I knew in my heart the attraction differed because I had changed. My choices wouldn't be the same. If we fell in love, it would be an occurrence for me to cherish rather than waste with one foolish decision.

"I'm famished," he said, grabbing the two menus standing up, sandwiched between the salt and pepper shakers. "They have a rather swell cod fish and chips if you'd like a recommendation."

Fish and chips. Frankly, I couldn't remember the last time I had such an ordinary meal to enjoy. Living in a household with a French cook and meals with too many courses to count, it sounded deliciously fun.

"I like that idea," I said. "Order me what you're having."

A waitress came to our table and placed two glasses of water before us. "Have you decided what you'd like for lunch?" She smiled a Reginald, barely taking notice of me. I couldn't blame her because he did look rather dashing.

"We'll have two orders of cod fish and chips," he said.

"Cod," she said, writing down the order on her pad. "Anything to drink?"

"What would like, Isabella?"

"Tea would be all right," I answered.

"I'll have Barclay's ale."

"Coming up," the perky waitress responded.

"Hope you don't mind my having a drink," Reginald said apologetically.

"No, not at all. It probably goes great with the fish batter," I teased. "Don't they sometimes make beer batter?"

"They do, but the alcohol dissipates when they fry the fish."

"Ah," I responded, having no idea about beer batter deep-fry cooking.

The waitress returned with our drinks. While I added milk to my tea, Reginald appeared anxious for his first frothy gulp. He took one and then set the glass down on the table.

"So what have you been up to?" he asked, glancing at my bags. "It appears you purchased a few new frocks." He teasingly peeked into one of them.

"Yes, dresses. Father has given me an allowance to buy a new wardrobe." I hesitated for a moment and then asked him a silly question. "What is your favorite color?" His left brow rose above his eye, which I had never noticed before. It was an endearing ability to raise one eyebrow and leave the other in the same place.

"Oh, I don't know," he said. "Men never think about things like that." After looking into the two bags, he commented on my choices. "It appears you like light blue and shades of purple." He glanced over at me with a sly grin. "Should go well with your hair color." After slurping a quick drink, he looked at me thoughtfully. "Are they for a special occasion?"

"The blue one is for my attendance at the Royal Ascot." When I made the announcement, I felt a tinge of embarrassment. I wondered, of course, if he had ever attended.

"You'll need some fancy hat to go with it then." He grinned. "I suppose with feathers, flowers, and all the other adornments."

Wanting to change the subject, I took a sip of tea. "So you saw my father today?"

"Yes, as a matter of fact."

"Does he see you often?"

"Often enough." He pulled his eyes away as if he were avoiding the conversation.

"About what?" I pried.

He tilted his head and gave me a cautionary look. "Isabella, you know I cannot break solicitor confidentiality with a client."

Of course I knew but wanted to test him, regardless.

"I hope I didn't cause any trouble by calling your home," my voice asked sheepishly.

"No, Esther, my nanny, wasn't sure if it was important, so she telephoned me at work to let me know." He paused and took another sip of ale. "If I have a private moment in my office, I can always telephone you back. But like I said, calling me there isn't the best."

"Understandable," I assured him. "Of course, calling me at my home isn't the best either." My lips puffed a sigh. "It makes it difficult to communicate."

"It does." He pondered with downcast eyes.

"I heard a screaming child in the background when I called." It was impossible not to mention.

"Screaming?" He chuckled aloud. "Yes, that would be my little one."

Reginald used a generic reference, not giving me the gender. It didn't defuse my interest, and my heart swelled affectionately. Thankfully, the waitress approached the table with our order. Otherwise, I think I would have overwhelmed him with nosey questions. It didn't take long for him to dig in to his meal, acting as if he didn't wish to discuss the matter further. There would be other occasions, of that I felt assured. Today, though, I just wanted to enjoy my time with him and not be an intrusive companion.

The aroma of the fish and chips wafted toward my nose, and I picked up the fork to take a bite.

"Not like that," he said, grabbing a chip and shoving it in his mouth. "You must enjoy the experience of eating chips with your fingers."

My upbringing had turned me into a formal eater as I watched him chomp away at his food. If I had dared to pick up anything with my fingers during dinner at our house, I would have received a hard wallop and sent to bed hungry.

"All right then," I said, grabbing a chip. The greasy fried potato steamed, and as I bit into it, I thought for sure I had burned my tongue.

"You might want to blow on it first," he said. "Cool it off."

"I'm such a ninny," I admitted, looking at the dangling chip clutched between my forefinger and thumb.

"You'll get used to it. Your father

probably wouldn't approve of my corrupting dining influence on you." He laughed aloud.

"Well, I don't care," I said, shoving the chip in my mouth and savoring each bite. It was quite good. "They need a bit of salt," I said, grabbing the shaker and giving it a few taps. Feeling like a pro, I picked up two the next time and chewed on the tasty morsel. Reginald ate but kept his eyes on me obviously enjoying my newfound amusement at the pub.

After we had devoured our lunch together, I worried that our precious time had begun to slip away. I caught him glancing at the clock on the wall a few times, indicating he had to get back to work soon.

"Can we do this again?" My suggestion sounded a bit desperate.

"Yes, I'd like that," he replied.

The waitress interrupted us for a moment to clear our table and leave the bill. She stepped away, and Reginald's hand slipped across the table and touched me tenderly.

"You are a sweet lady." His thumb drew little circles on the back of my hand. "It's my hope, Isabella, that we can see each other often." After pausing and sucking in a breath, he spoke. "I enjoy being in your company."

His words warmed my heart. "I'm so glad," I gushed. "Being with you makes me happy. I feel like a normal human being accepted for whom I am."

"You'll be gone next week to Berkshire, I take it."

I nodded affirmatively. "Frankly, I'm quite anxious that my parents wish to throw me into social circles in the hopes of catching a husband." The thought made me shudder that their actions could keep me from Reginald.

"Well, they love you and want the best," he quietly replied.

"You are the best," I whispered. My heart didn't want to look elsewhere when the man who had charmed me sat a few feet away still holding my hand. His mouth turned upward into a weak smile while I considered the obstacles between us.

"Call me when you are back." he said, "And we'll figure out a way to get together again." With a quick squeeze, he let go of my hand and rose to his feet. "I must be going."

Reginald handed me the parcels. He paid the tab, and we walked outdoors and halted on the sidewalk, standing face-to-face.

"Better go find that hat. Make it an outrageous one," he said.

He eyed me adoringly, which gave me hope that our relationship was growing. Unable to control myself, I glanced at his lips. When he saw my action, he put his finger against them and then kissed me softly on my right cheek.

"Good-bye, Isabella."

My eyes followed him as he walked down the street and hailed a cab to take him back to the office. When he disappeared, I knew then that I had begun to fall in love.

ELEVEN

HATS AND HORSES

My first Royal Ascot had arrived, but no royalty attended. Perhaps fate had added it to my punishment so that I wouldn't enjoy my arrival into society as much as I should have. When father told me that King Edward VIII would not attend, my heart sank to the floor. Of course, the nation had lost King George VI in January and mourning lingered. Nevertheless, no one mourned at the Ascot when it came to fashion and hats.

The first two days of the affair had become a whirlwind of ceremonies, horse races, and fine food. Father and Mother dragged me around, reminding me that my status as excess baggage remained. Soon I became bored with introductions, petty conversations, and the glaring sun that had begun to burn my fair skin in my short-sleeve chiffon.

On the day of the Gold Cup, there had

been an early morning shower, but by the midafternoon, the sun had reappeared. Thankfully, a light breeze cooled my face but hadn't blown my hat off into the field. Reginald was quite right about my preferences. After we had parted from our luncheon, I spent a good hour at the millinery shop, trying on at least a dozen choices. I returned home with an ivory brimmed hat, trimmed with a wide taupe ribbon, and pheasant tail feathers swirling off to the side. It was the perfect choice for my outfit.

On the third day, we attended Ladies' Day because my father was most interested in the Golden Cup. Even though I enjoyed horses, the races were a frenzy of pounding hooves, turf flying in the air, and loud onlookers cheering for their favorite horse. Before the race started, I wandered off for a moment by myself. The landscape of finely dressed ladies with a sea of top hats offered plenty to take in. As I halted to look at the schedule for the day, I glanced up to see Mother heading my way with a gentleman by her side. Instantly I knew an introduction would be forthcoming, so I inhaled a deep breath for fortitude.

"Isabella." My mother called my name and halted in front of me.

"Mother."

"Lord Ridley has expressed his interest in an introduction," she cheerfully announced.

"Really?" My eyes shifted toward the gentleman. He tipped his hat and flashed me a pearly smile.

"Lord Ridley, this is my daughter Isabella," she announced with a feigned prideful tone.

"Lady Isabella. It's a pleasure to meet you."

His lordship's voice sounded like a squeaky hinge that instantly grated upon my ears. My thoughts turned to Reginald's velvet tone, wishing he were standing with me instead.

"The pleasure is all mine," I responded. The idiotic words flew out of my mouth from finishing school. Mother grinned at me, and I saw her intent to abandon us to get to know one another.

"Well, I'll leave you alone to chat," she said.

After nodding at him, which I considered being her latest offering to push me toward the altar, she disappeared back into the crowd. My stomach tightened as my eyes moved slowly in the direction of the gentleman.

"Are you enjoying yourself?" he asked. "I say, fine weather it turned out to be."

He took a step closer, and I stepped back. "Somewhat," I coldly replied. "This is my first time, so the entire affair has been an education, to say the least."

"Indeed," he drawled. "I attend every year, hoping one day to have my own horse in the race."

As hard as I attempted to look him straight in the eye, I found it impossible. His features were pleasant, albeit I thought him too short for my taste. He had wavy blond hair, dark blue eyes, and his physical characteristics exuded aristocratic snobbery. Trying not to pay close attention to him, my eyes glanced over his shoulder into the grandstand. Suddenly I wanted to yelp in glee. There stood Reginald in the distance, watching me. After my heart thumped against my chest, I could only do one thing.

"I do beg your pardon," my words gasped. "It was nice meeting you, but I have somewhere else that I need to be."

Without waiting for his reaction or a word to leave his lips, I pushed passed the gentleman and headed toward Reginald. The annoying crowd kept me from a sprint, and after multiple "excuse me" moments of pushing my way forward, I was close enough to wave.

"Reginald!" My hand lifted in the air, and he grinned boyishly at my antics. Because he could not enter the Royal Enclosure, I managed to wiggle my way into the grandstand. After a very unladylike climb over the barrier, I nearly fell at his feet.

"Oh, dear Reginald, it is so good to see you! What are you doing here?" Out of breath and excited, my face burst into a cheeky smile. He looked at me with equal enthusiasm.

"I'm so glad I caught your eye," he said. "Frankly, I didn't think I'd be able to see you in the crowd."

"You didn't tell me you were coming

when we last spoke," I said, giving him a slight squeeze of his forearm.

"Well, to be honest, since I couldn't share it with you in the Royal Enclosure, I didn't think it would matter."

"It does matter," I chided him. "I don't need to be in there with all the stuffy crowd. It will be just fine standing here with you by my side."

At that moment, they announced that the race would soon start. I could see in the distance the horses lining up at the starting line.

"Do you have a favorite to win?" he asked.

"Well, you'll need to educate me, because I don't have a clue about who is who on four legs."

"I'm betting on Quashed," he announced. "She's a great filly. But most think that Omaha, an American horse, will win. He's pretty unbeatable."

"Well, I will cheer on your choice." It felt natural to loop my arm around his as we stood to wait.

"It's a two-and-a-half-mile race. Let's hope he keeps his stamina," Reginald added.

As he finished his statement, the battle to the finish line began. "What number is he?" All I could see was a jumble of horseflesh speeding down the grassy track. Reginald had a small pair of binoculars and quickly immersed himself in the rousing scene. In fact, the entire crowd of a hundred thousand individuals turned their heads to watch.

Of course, I had no idea where the horse was in the mix of the others. Nevertheless, I joined in the occasional "go Quashed" shouts while standing close to Reginald who bellowed the steed's name.

"What's happening?" I asked, trying to get Reginald's attention.

"It's close."

After another minute, the crowd raised their voices in a frenzy and the horses headed for the finish line. "Come on Quashed," Reginald cheered. "Come on!"

As the horses came into view, I could finally see the number identifying Omaha, who was running side by side to Quashed. As he crossed the line where the finish post stood, it looked like a tie to me.

"Who won?" I entreated, grabbing his

forearm.

"Not sure," Reginald said a little more subdued. Need to wait and see. A minute later, a pennant hoisted up a pole showing the number of Quashed, and the crowd went wild. The British had beaten the Americans by a nose.

"Wow, talk about close," I reacted. Reginald suddenly threw his arms around my waist and hoisted me in the air like the flag, swirling me around in a circle.

"He won!"

Then he set me down on two feet, lowered his head, and planted a kiss on my lips that took my breath away. My head went dizzy, my knees grew weak, and I nearly fainted in the man's tight embrace. As if he suddenly realized what he had spontaneously done, he drew back wide-eyed.

"I'm sorry, Isabella," he said. "Quite cheeky of me, I'm afraid, to steal a kiss like that."

"Steal another," I pleaded. A smile curled his lips, and he pulled me close. My body molded next to his and fit perfectly. The moistness of his lips and tenderness of his kiss showed me what he held in his heart, and I felt it too. We were falling in love.

It should have been a perfect moment, but as life had shown me in the past, nothing would be easy.

"Isabella!"

My mother's undeniable shrieking voice met my ears. As soon as I heard it, I pulled away from Reginald and stepped backward. When I did, he put more space between us and turned pale as the grandstand behind him.

"Let me handle this, Reginald. You need not get involved."

"But I am involved," he replied. "This affects both of us."

"Please," I pleaded. "Mother will feed you to the horses. I know how to appease her wrath."

Reginald conceded and nodded. I gave his hand a quick squeeze and then approached my mother.

"I'm coming," I yelled. Once again, I made a rather unladylike maneuver, returning to the enclosure. Without hesitation, I grabbed her by the arm and led her away. "You may spill your displeasure elsewhere but not in front of Reginald." Surprised that I even had the gall to speak to her like that gave me empowerment to face the impending hell. Mother wiggled out of my grasp.

"Let go of me," she growled. "What do you think you were doing, young lady, kissing that man in public?"

"We were celebrating the win," my nonchalant words replied. "Nothing more."

"I leave you with Lord Ridley, and you climb into the grandstand like a commoner. I'm warning you, Isabella. . ."

"Or what?" I replied, stopping in the middle of the crowd. "You and Father will send me off to another finishing school on the Continent? I'm a grown woman now, and I can make my choices."

"We'll see about that." She huffed. "Your rudeness to Lord Ridley is unforgivable."

When I had returned to my father's presence, I tried to make light of the situation. "Did your horse win, Father?"

He shook his head and scowled. "No, lost by a nose."

After hearing the news, I wanted to

make a snide remark but held my words. I had no idea why he would gamble on an American horse but apparently thought it unbeatable like many other spectators.

"I see your mother has retrieved you from your wanderings," he commented, narrowing his eyes. "We'll discuss it when we get home. I'm in no mood at the moment."

After that remark, he walked in front of us, expecting Mother and me to follow along. It was time to return to the estate and face my latest chastisement. The lingering taste of Reginald upon my lips would give me the strength to stand my ground.

My eyes darted toward the grandstand, but I could no longer see his handsome face.

TWELVE

LINES ARE DRAWN

Perhaps I had been foolish to think that I would be allowed to do as I pleased. The displeasure upon the faces of my parents haunted me the trip home though nothing of essence had been spoken. Father stared out the window, no doubt ruminating over Omaha's loss of the race, making me wonder if he had lost a tidy sum. Mother, on the other hand, bore her beady eyes of anger in my direction, which for the most part I successfully ignored.

After we had arrived home, we all disbursed our separate ways while the servants brought in our luggage. Father off to his study. Mother to the parlor, barking orders for tea. When I turned to climb the stairs, her crackling voice called after me.

"Isabella, I wish a word with you."

Hesitant and not in the mood, I slowly turned around to face her. "Can this wait until later? I am tired and wish a bath." Mother glared at me and then relented.

"Fine. No doubt your father shall wish to join the discussion. Meet us here in the parlor a half hour before the gong sounds for dinner."

The gong. I wanted to walk over, grab the hammer, and hit the damn thing a thousand times out of frustration.

"Well, why don't we send for Father and get this over with," I suggested. "No use putting off the inescapable."

Mother's eyes widened at my brashness. As the maid entered with a tray of tea and biscuits, she took me up on my offer.

"Mildred, would you be so kind as to ask his lordship to join us in the parlor for tea? I believe you can find him in the study."

"Yes, your ladyship."

After a quick curtsy, she departed to do her task, and I sat down in a single chair across from Mother. A few moments later, Father arrived looking displeased at the summons.

"You wish to see me?"

"Yes, dear, have a seat," Mother said. She quickly rose, walked over to the parlor door, and shut it.

"What's this about?" Father asked, glancing back and forth at the two of us.

"About my behavior," I quickly interjected, not wishing to give Mother an upper hand. "She no doubt wants to tell you that she caught me kissing Reginald Spencer in the grandstand after the race this afternoon."

"You what?" my father hollered, flashing a harsh glare.

"Precisely," Mother countered. "Shameless behavior in public. I quickly removed her from the situation."

"Now wait a minute," I protested, glowering at her in return. "If I remember right, it was I who willingly removed myself, grabbed your arm, and led you away."

"I am not the one on trial here," she quipped in return.

"Trial?" I shook my head and laughed. "So that's it. Are you going to punish me again by sending me away?"

"Well, let me settle this once and for all," Father announced. "Might I ask what is going on between you and Reginald?"

"He's a friend." I lifted my chin, showing no embarrassment. "When he escorted me home from France, we formed a friendship of sorts."

"Well, if he's kissed you, obviously he wants something more," Father gruffly concluded.

"Perhaps." After a short pause, I explained it away. "His horse won, and in his excitement, he just kissed me in a celebratory fashion."

"Well, it didn't look like that to me," Mother countered with a huff. "You had your arms around his neck and were kissing him in return."

"I enjoyed it. Reginald is a nice man."

"As long as that's the end of it," Father said matter-of-factly. "There is to be no consorting between the two of you any further."

"And if there is, then what?" Naturally, I had to press the matter but gulped afterward.

"Then I will be forced to make an unpleasant decision, Isabella, which could harm his career." He shot a threatening glare in my direction.

"You wouldn't," I countered, narrowing my eyes. "How could you do something so cruel?"

"He's not for you," Mother added. "Lord Ridley has an interest in you, Isabella. In spite of your spurning of the gentleman earlier today, he has invited us to dinner."

How drab and dull. The thought of vomiting in his soup crossed my mind. The scheme would be perfect for the gentleman to corner me in an attempt to woo my affections.

"I shall not attend," I firmly announced while squirming in my seat. "You may apologize for my absence and make up some story about my being ill."

Father rose, took a step forward, and towered above me. "You will go, young lady, and I shall hear nothing more of your complaining. We have made our wishes known, and I fully expect your compliance as long as you live under my roof."

"Or what, you'll kick me out?" I asked, jumping up to face him. My brash actions surprised me. As I glared back at my father, the nerves in my fingers tingled. Father shook his head at me in disappointment.

Apparently, I had not returned as finished as he hoped.

"You exasperate me," he growled. "You were born and bred to be a lady, yet you insist on acting like a child. This discussion is over." He flung open the parlor door and stormed down the hallway. After he had left, I glanced over at Mother.

"I wouldn't push your father, Isabella. He makes no veiled threats. If you disobey, you will pay for it dearly. Of that, I am sure."

A hard knot grasped my stomach. Unable to reply, I merely spun around and left Mother with the tepid tea. Reginald had been quite right. Our affections would not be readily accepted by my parents. Nevertheless, I wasn't about to give up this easily.

There were two telephones in our household, one in my father's study and the other in the parlor from where I had just left. Calling Reginald would be a challenge, but I intended to do so as soon as I could without my parents' notice. The unfair situation angered me. Surely there had to be a way to follow my heart rather than a path chosen by my family. After all, this was the

1930s and not the Victorian era.

The opportunity to call Reginald never arrived before our engagement. On the contrary, I felt as if the phones had been guarded because they anticipated my intentions. Before I could find the opportunity to speak with him, the evening of our dinner invitation arrived.

My parents and I barely exchanged a word the entire trip to Lord Ridley's estate. Attempts to manipulate my life to their whims and desires only increased my waning affections for them further.

As the motorcar pulled up to the residence, I glanced at the massive stone edifice. Mother watched for my response, which I refused to give her by speaking of the grand manor house. Perhaps she thought I would be impressed and wish it to be mine one day. I had to admit it stirred my admiration, reminding me of a dangling carrot in front of my nose.

Upon our entrance into the foyer, Lord Ridley approached with a smile on his face and welcoming demeanor. At first he paid attention to my parents, no doubt showing his respect to stay on their good side. When he turned and glanced at me, I noted the glint of sincerity in his eyes.

"Lady Isabella, welcome." His squeaky voice left much to be desired. When he glanced at my hand, I raised it, which he promptly took and gave it a peck upon my knuckles. I considered it old-fashion rather than romantic as if I were ushered into some odd, dreamy novel, attempting to pull me into a story. Finally, after my jumbled thoughts had ceased, I spoke a weak, "Thank you." Lord Ridley smirked as if he were up for the challenge.

"Dinner will be announced soon," he said, gesturing toward the large sitting room off to the left.

As I followed him into the ostentatious surroundings, my eyes glanced back and forth at the décor. His manor was much like our dated residence, filled with relics of generations past and portraits of ancestors hanging on its walls. Mother had already advised me that he had inherited the estate upon his father's passing a few years ago. It made me wonder how he survived alone, except for his staff, in the rambling empty hallways and rooms that encircled him daily.

As we sat for a few minutes before dinner, I desperately attempted to remain aloof. My eyes scanned my surroundings and successfully tuned out the conversation occurring between Lord Ridley and my father. My mother's cold steel gaze could be felt from a few feet away. Nervously I fiddled with my dress skirt, smoothing out a wrinkle with my hand.

"And how are you enjoying your return home from the Continent?" Lord Ridley asked, pulling my attention toward him.

"Enjoyable," I responded. One word had been the only thing I felt like saying.

"Could you elaborate?" he countered.

By the look in his eye and tone of his voice, he refused to let me off easily with a short response. I decided to give him an entire sentence. "Both France and Switzerland were beautiful in landscape and the locals tolerable and kind." To my relief, dinner was announced, and we proceeded to the dining room.

We spent the next forty-five minutes having a leisurely meal. Lord Ridley often engaged with my parents, regarding topics involving current affairs and the changing political landscape in Europe. I, on the other hand, attempted to remain silent and demure only answering questions he posed. As the dinner drew to a close, he made a surprising move.

"I'd like to show Isabella our gardens," he announced. "Would you mind if I took her for a stroll among the roses?"

Naturally, I wanted to balk at his proposition. Father and Mother acted as if it were some well-planned ploy on their part. The suggestion, as far as I was concerned, bordered on rudeness to leave behind his guests for the singular purpose of spiriting me off alone.

"Oh, I don't think it proper to leave my parents alone," I whined, looking directly at Lord Ridley. "Where are your manners?" My question, which I had purposely composed to bring him shame, had no effect.

"Think nothing of it," Father interjected. "I'm sure Isabella would be delighted to take a stroll."

"I'd rather relax and have a cup of tea,"

my mother added with a sly smile.

"Very well then," Lord Ridley replied. "My butler shall show you to the drawing room and provide after-dinner drinks."

"Shall we?" Lord Ridley said, holding out his hand.

Placed in an impossible situation, I couldn't refuse. He pulled back my chair, and as I stood, I took his hand. As he directed me toward the veranda doors leading to the garden, he wrapped my arm around his but remained a respectable distance. His movements and swift abstraction of my presence from my parents annoyed me.

"I'm not interested," my voice squealed as soon as we stepped outdoors. The words flew from between my lips before I could stop them.

"I know," he replied nonchalantly.

My stride halted, and I pulled my arm from his. "Then you see, Lord Ridley, this entire affair has been orchestrated by my parents. Surely you feel as manipulated as I do."

"Well, not entirely," he scoffed. "I am a willing participant and do have a genuine interest in getting to know you."

He flashed his pearly teeth, and I had to admit the man oozed charisma, except for the tone of his speech. After exhaling a deep sigh of frustration, I gave him an honest reply.

"I'm afraid that my heart has been drawn in a different direction. My emotions are already intertwined with another man."

"So I've been told," he droned. "However, I've been given the impression by your parents that he is undesirable."

"Undesirable?" the pitch of my voice raised. "The man is intelligent, kind, and successful."

"But not an aristocrat," he pointedly remarked, beginning his stroll down the pebbled pathway through the garden.

Exasperated by his pretentious response, I refused to move. When he realized that I had not followed his lead, he stopped and turned around. His eyes ordered me onward. I knew it then that I had to put a stop to it before it went any further. After inhaling a deep breath, I spoke with determination.

"I'm not the kind of woman that an

aristocrat would be proud of having as his wife. There have been indiscretions in my past that could put your social standing at risk." My hand trembled as I declared my reasons. The word pregnancy lingered on the tip of my tongue, but I kept my mouth tightly shut. Should I dare to release that revelation, I would assuredly bring even more shame upon my parents.

Lord Ridley stood rigidly, contemplating my words, making me wonder if he had discerned exactly what my past held. Suddenly he took a stride forward and hovered over my body, causing me to lift my eyes to his.

"You mean the child you had out of wedlock?" he said in a low tone.

Shocked at his response, I sputtered, "You... you know?"

"Yes, I know." He smirked. "In spite of your indiscretions, I am still of the opinion that our coupling would be a congenial one."

Unable to move a muscle, I gaped at him in shock. "Who told you?"

His undesirable character sent a chill down my spine when I noted his cavalier attitude. "Your father mentioned it in private." His hand reached out and touched the side of my cheek, sliding his fingertips down to my lips. "However, I find you quite delightful as a young lady and would be pleased to have you in my bed."

"My father?" I couldn't believe he would do such a thing.

"I've known him for years," he added. "We have engaged in drinks and conversations at the gentleman's club in London. Let's just say he's been aware of my search for a wife and my less than stellar reputation, which keeps me from the cream of the crop, so to speak."

His admission produced visions of illicit affairs floating in my head, and heaven knows what else he had been engaged in. I wondered how many children he may have sired out of wedlock. It furthered my dislike of the man.

"And I suppose my father offered me up to you as of means of solving my problematic fallen state." My blood boiled over his conniving schemes.

"Yes, we came to a rather agreeable monetary arrangement."

"Monetary arrangement?" I couldn't believe what I was hearing. The blood drained from my face. "You mean he's paying you a dowry to marry me?"

"Perhaps it is an antiquated arrangement in the twentieth century, but my bank account could use a boost in this poor economy."

Immediately I jolted at his audacious remark as if I had been shocked by electricity. "You're a snake," I snarled. "You'll never have me in your bed." I turned to leave, but his hand wrapped around my upper arm preventing me from stepping away.

"I know things you do not, Isabella, including where that precious little girl of yours resides. Perhaps we can strike our own arrangement."

His announcement of my daughter's whereabouts sucked the breath out of my lungs. "Where... where is she?"

"I'm not about to play that card so swiftly," he coolly replied. "Let us agree that you have something that I want and I have something that you want."

All of a sudden I saw it as an evil ploy on

his behalf to win my attentiveness. "You're lying," I scoffed, backing away. "You're trying to trick me." I began stomping down the path toward the house, my heart pounding furiously in my chest.

"She's still in London," he called after me. His voice remained calm and confident. "You have probably passed her on the street with a hundred other children and never knew she belonged to you."

The torturous words halted my steps, and he slithered up to my side. "You see, I find you most endearing as a young lady regardless of your past." He smirked. "My own indiscretions makes us a rather worthy pair."

His eyes penetrated my soul as if he were undressing me to consummate the marriage. Had my parents any idea of the kind of evil creature they had chosen?

"I'll make an attentive husband." His assuring voice enticed. "You will want for nothing financially or emotionally." A wicked smile curled the corner of his mouth. "And may I add physically?" His eyes wandered down toward my breasts and lingered. "And I'll shower you with expensive jewelry to replace the trinkets you wear."

He glanced at my locket in distaste, but I said nothing about the sentimentality or its contents. The man had emotionally cornered me, clouding my mind. My eyes searched his, looking for truth as to whether he knew where my daughter resided. An unquenchable urge to see her welled in my heart. But at what price? I had fallen in love with Reginald. Now this man, whom I loathed, had given me hope that I might see my daughter.

"Does my father agree with you, regarding this ploy to tell me of my daughter's whereabouts after we wed? Was it his idea?"

He burst out laughing. "Oh, dear God, no. I'd be a fool to expose my methods to him at this point in the game. He swore me to secrecy on pain of death, but he doesn't realize that I can be as sly as he is in his old age. What transpires between the two of us is not his business." The squeak in his voice had turned deeply threatening.

"Is she well?" My voice trembled to know the answer. He merely grinned.

"I would like to take you to the opera Friday evening," he replied, ignoring my question. "It should give us time alone to get to know one another."

"If I agree, will you answer my question?"

"Perhaps."

"Don't trifle with my emotions, Lord Ridley." I hissed in anger. "Your little game is irritating, and if I find out you are lying to me, I will—"

"I'm not lying, Isabella. You can be assured that I have your interests at heart as well as mine."

He lowered his head and kissed me on my cheek and whispered, "Give me a chance."

I had been rendered helpless and could not deny his request. If he knew where Mary Jane lived, I had to discover her whereabouts.

"All right then. Friday evening."

Finally I found the strength to continue toward the veranda and return indoors. Having received from me what he wanted, Lord Ridley gave no objection. We returned to the sitting room. My parents sat quietly chatting with drinks in their hands. As soon as I entered, I made my request.

"Father, I'd like to leave if we could. I'm feeling a bit under the weather." I dragged the back of my hand across my forehead and grimaced as if I had a headache. To be honest, one had started thanks to my recent conversation with Lord Ridley.

"Are you sure?" Mother inquired.

"I understand fully if Lady Isabella needs to retire," Lord Ridley agreed. He flashed an empathic glance in my direction.

"Well, all right then," Father replied, rising to his feet.

"Your daughter has agreed to accompany me to the opera Friday," he announced, glancing at me affectionately.

"Delightful," Mother replied.

Sickened by my parents' noticeable pleasure that I would accompany the dark lord, as I now thought of him, I couldn't help but sneer inwardly.

"Thank you for dinner," I said, turning to go.

"Thank you," Lord Ridley replied. "Until Friday."

He reached out and kissed my hand

once again. Perhaps I should have heard music playing in the background. Instead, my stomach growled in protest.

By the end of his good-bye, I had had enough of the man. Nearly running to the door, I flung it open before the footman had done so and ran out into the courtyard. All I wanted to do was get as far away as possible from him and my despicable Father, who plotted to sell me to another man.

THIRTEEN

DESPERATE MEASURES

There are advantages to having loyal staff who have watched you grow up from childhood. Occasionally they are willing to help when needed, and such is the case with Giles, our butler. The following morning, as if Reginald knew in his heart I needed to hear from him, a posted letter arrived. After mail had been delivered, each morning our butler gave the entire stack of letters to my father. If something were among the arriving correspondence addressed to another, he would be the one to divvy the post if he saw fit. Of course, anything from Reginald would have no doubt been confiscated if it had my name as the addressee.

Giles, apparently privy to all the conversations of the household had, as any good servant, kept silent in the background. It wasn't until recently that I realized he had harbored empathy for me, regarding my choices in male companionship. As I came down to breakfast, he cornered me in the hall and slipped the envelope into my hand.

"This came for you in the morning delivery," he whispered. "I thought it only fair that I should deliver it directly to you." He winked affectionately, accenting the crow's-feet around his eyes. He had, after twenty years of service, entered his elder years. Having never known him to disobey an order in the household, my heart swelled with gratitude at the gesture.

"Giles, you are a dear," I replied. "Thank you so much." I shoved the letter into my skirt pocket and grinned my gratefulness from ear to ear.

"You are most welcome, Lady Isabella. I shall be pleased to do so again in the future if called upon."

He turned and left with the stack of envelopes, heading for my father at the breakfast table to deliver the mail. I, on the other hand, headed in the opposite direction back toward my room for a moment of privacy. After locking my door, I sat on a chair by my window and slipped the envelope open with my finger.

Anxiously pulling out the correspondence, I held it in my trembling hands.

"*My dearest, Isabella. . .*"

Dearest, he calls me dearest, and my heart swells.

"*It is with great regret and sorrow that I pen this message to you. Recently it has been brought to my attention that our association and friendship is a conflict of interest in my current position as solicitor for your father. Our firm has represented his legal needs for over twenty years. As our senior partner has reminded me, the satisfaction of our clientele is paramount. Any personal desires that I may hold in continuing our friendship, which may contain romantic notions as I'm told, must cease.*

As of this morning, I have been sternly advised to break our personal rapport immediately. If I do not, there will be consequences up to and including my dismissal of employment.

Please be assured that I hold you in the highest regard and wish you every happiness in the future.

Sincerely,

Reginald"

By the time I finished the letter, I had crushed it between my fingers. Tears of sorrow, laced with underlying anger, trickled down my cheeks. In my heart, I knew that Reginald did not wish us to part. Nevertheless, my father must have interfered and put his foot down as he had warned. Hatred for my parents consumed me to such an extent that I feared I would run downstairs and stab my father with the cutlery on the breakfast table.

Undeterred and defiant, I wiped my tears from my cheeks. The letter found a place in the bottom of my dresser drawer underneath my slips. After powdering my nose again, I descended the stairs to join my family for breakfast. Two can play this game, I thought to myself. And play it to the end, I would.

"Good morning," I gleefully announced, heading for the sideboard and grabbing a plate. Father sat, going through the morning mail. Needless to say, I loathed the despicable man. After filling my plate with food, I sat down, flipped open the linen napkin, and placed it on my lap.

"I've been thinking," I stated. "If you wish me to make a good impression at the opera this Friday with Lord Ridley, a new evening gown might do the trick." Instantly that comment perked my mother's ears that I should suggest enticing the man with a new frock. Father, who never remained quiet when money was mentioned, took no time answering after considering the merits of my suggestion.

"I have no objection. You may charge it to my account, but don't overdo it," he warned.

"Thank you. May I have the driver take me into town around eleven?"

"Do you wish to accompany Isabella?" My father glanced at my mother, suggesting to ruin everything.

"Oh dear," she sighed. "I'm afraid that my lady's bridge club meets this morning here at our home."

Too blind to see any untoward motives on my part, she relented.

"You may take the car and go. Will you be seeing our usual dressmaker?"

"Yes, no doubt," I replied. "However, if I find nothing to my liking, I may try a few other shops."

Father placed his hand inside his vest and pulled out his wallet. To my shock, he opened it and grabbed fifty pounds, handing it over to me.

"Here, take this in case you need anything else." He held out the crisp notes.

Devil, I thought to myself. He is going to shower me with clothes and money to purchase my willingness to court the snake. The two of them were in cahoots regarding my future, which bordered on criminal. My mother appeared to be uninformed, but I wondered about her involvement too. Naturally, I grabbed the offering without guilt.

"Thank you," I said demurely. "It's very kind of you to offer." I folded the bills and shoved them in my skirt pocket that had recently held Reginald's letter. Little did my parents know that I planned to break the barrier between the two of us while dress shopping. Frankly, I felt gleefully wicked.

As I paced up and down the street, keeping an eye on the firm's office door, I anticipated that Reginald would eventually leave for lunch. For my daring plot to work, I prayed earnestly that he would be alone rather than eat with a coworker. My wristwatch had just moved its hand toward noon. Inwardly, I despaired he would appear. I halted for a moment, wringing my hands in worry, when the door flew open and Reginald bounced down the stoop to the sidewalk. He turned toward the left unaware that I stood only a few yards away. As he traversed the crowded walkway, I gained distance until we strode side by side.

"Hello, Reginald." Naturally, I could not contain the giddy smile spreading across my face. He halted in his step when he heard my voice.

"Isabella!"

A mixture of surprise and fear flashed in his gaze, which caused me to doubt the wisdom of my actions. The last thing I wanted to do was cause him trouble.

"What are you doing here?"

He glanced around at the people surrounding us as we stood still in the midst of a rambling crowd, appearing fearful that we might be seen together.

"I needed to see you," my voice

quavered.

"Didn't you receive my letter?"

"Yes, of course, but—"

His eyes darted over my shoulder, and alarm spread across his face. He grabbed me by the arm and pulled me through the door of a nearby flower shop. With apprehension etched across his face, he watched another male pass by the door.

"That was close." His chest heaved. "Our clerk could have seen us together."

Reginald turned his attention to me, and I wanted to throw my arms around his neck and kiss him until my lips swelled. The aroma of the flower shop's blooms filled my nostrils, sending romantic notions swirling through my head.

"May I help you?" A voice from behind the counter inquired as a result of our sudden presence. A small, stout, middle-aged woman smiled in our direction.

"What should we do?" I whispered.

"Purchase a bouquet," he answered quietly. "Seems only natural."

"Oh, I couldn't take it." I knew if I returned with flowers, my parents would question me relentlessly. Besides, I still needed to shop, and carrying around a dozen red roses in my arms would be rather awkward.

"Just one," I replied. "Purchase one red rose for me to take away and tell me there is still hope that we will be together." My desperation needed a sign.

"How can there be?" Reginald whispered in my ear. He looked at the clerk and implored her absence. "Would you excuse us for a moment?"

"Yes, of course," she replied. "I have things to do in the back room." She grinned at the two of us as if she were watching a romantic dalliance play out before her eyes.

When she disappeared, I turned toward him. "Reginald," I pleaded. "I do not wish to part."

"Neither do I." He reached out and grabbed my hand, holding it tightly between his cold fingers. "But darling, the choice has been made and we must."

"My father threatened your livelihood. He told me would," my voice boomed. "I hate the man."

"Don't," he said. Reginald brought his hand to my cheek and glided his fingertips across my skin. "He has his reasons."

"What reasons? He wishes me to marry an aristocrat. This is the twentieth century, for heaven's sake, not the past where a woman had no voice in the matters of the heart." My lungs heaved, rapidly inhaling air as I spewed my displeasure. Reginald, on the other hand, appeared resigned to our plight and calmer.

"Let us meet in secret," I beseeched. "What harm can it do?"

"I've been told that your engagement is pending with Lord Ridley," he sadly remarked. His gaze pulled away as if it hurt to admit the announcement.

"Yes, my parents desire it, and the snake wishes it." I seethed in disgust. My hand began to tremble in Reginald's as he continued to hold it tightly.

"Snake?" he asked quizzically.

"I think he's a snake, and I have no desire to be his wife. Nevertheless, he. . ." My thought shifted into silence, holding back the secret he professed to hold. Surely Reginald would think me a foolish woman to be manipulated as such.

"Darling, you should do as your parents

require of you," he admonished me in a fatherly tone. "They have your best interests at heart. Besides. . ." He halted his words and gazed into my eyes longingly. "The responsibilities I bear between work and home make it difficult to pursue a courtship."

My heart sank into an abyss of despair. "You don't mean that," I protested. "You love me, and I love you."

"Isabella," he breathed from his lips, imploring me to understand.

Not caring who witnessed my actions, I flung my arms around Reginald and kissed him ardently. My body and soul ached for him. An undeniable connection between the two of our hearts existed, and no matter how much he protested, it could not be denied.

Rather than resisting me in return, Reginald passionately responded. His kissed me deeply, and I felt my strength drain from my body as if I were at his mercy to do with me as he pleased even in a flower shop. My heart adored him, and I wanted to be his wife. He pulled away from my lips, gazing at me as if he were in agony too.

"I adore you; you know I do," he muttered, sounding tragically poetic.

Unable to commit further with words of love, he turned toward the counter. The clerk reappeared from behind a door, smirking at the two of us.

"One long-stem red rose, with a white ribbon," he ordered.

Reginald pulled out a few quid from his wallet and handed it over. In return, she gave him a perfectly bloomed flower, with a bow tied around its stem. When he handed it to me, my heart leaped in my chest.

"Darling, this is all I can give you at the moment as a token of my love, but I can hardly give you any hope of a future."

My trembling hand reached out and took the rose, clutching it to my chest. "Please, Reginald, let us see one another when we can," I implored him.

He lowered his head in disappointment. "I cannot in good conscience encourage or agree to a duplicitous relationship. It does you, your parents, and even Lord Ridley dishonor."

"Oh, Reginald," I groaned. "Don't. . ."

"I must go," he said. He put his hands on my shoulders and kissed my cheek as if I were a little girl in need of assurance rather than the woman he intimately longed to make love to.

"Will I see you again?" I asked on the verge of tears.

"I cannot say," he replied indifferently. With those words, he flung open the door and sprinted down the sidewalk out of sight.

Too distraught to move, I remained standing by the door, clutching the rose. Even though all the thorns had been clipped from the stem, I felt as if one had lodged painfully in my heart.

"If it's any consolation," the clerk said, "it is clear to me the man is besotted with you."

"Perhaps," I whimpered. "But we cannot be together."

"Don't despair," she assured me. "Love often wins."

"Thank you," I mumbled.

With a rose in hand, I stepped out into the fresh air, glancing to my left and right. Reginald had disappeared. Now alone and with money in my purse, I had the awful task of dress shopping for my engagement with Lord Ridley. The onerous task would not be an easy one. In a daze, I headed for the dress shop with a bleeding heart and reddened eyes.

FOURTEEN

THE OUT-OF-TUNE ARIA

There I was, sitting in a box at the Royal Opera House, attempting to enjoy my evening. Adorned in an expensive new evening gown, I had to admit that I looked stunning. Lord Ridley, who now insisted that I address him as Edward, repeatedly complimented me on my new finery. When Father saw the bill, though, he showed less pleasure. Perhaps I did spend a tidy sum, thinking it apt punishment for his manipulation. Regrettably, I had come to the snarly conclusion that most men were schemers. Even Reginald had attempted to influence me to do the right thing.

When intermission arrived, I rose to my feet to stretch my legs. My intentions were to run to the ladies' powder room and spend the next twenty minutes hiding from my escort. Edward apparently had other things in mind.

"Stay," he said, reaching out and

grabbing my hand. "I wish to talk."

"About what?" I flashed a disgruntled look, conveying my annoyance. Ignoring me, he pulled me back until I felt forced to sit again.

"Talk with me," he implored. "We have spent hours together already this evening, and you have barely uttered two sentences."

I had been overly quiet and uninterested in Edward's company. My mind would not stop thinking of Reginald. Nevertheless, having been schooled to be a lady, I had to admit that my behavior bordered on rudeness.

"I apologize," I said, straining to keep eye contact with him.

"You are struggling. I understand," he said. "If you would just surrender, Isabella, you would feel more at ease," he entreated in a softly spoken tone. It did nothing to help his raspy squeak of a voice.

Surrender? I stiffened instead. I didn't wish to give in to his advances. All I wanted was Reginald, but the gulf between us loomed even wider as I sat there with no other options to pursue. Regardless of how kind and attentive Edward had played his part, I felt we were out of tune on so many levels. The aristocrat before me had nothing that I wanted, except one thing.

"Do you really know where she is?"

The charm he had wielded earlier evaporated. His eyes grew dark as he warily looked at me. Underneath his tender pretense, I saw an exasperated man.

"And if I told you, would that make any difference?"

"What do you mean?"

"Would you allow me to love and marry you?"

He studied my reaction, but I merely recoiled at the thought.

"She is closer than you think," he said, teasing me even further.

In my mind's eye, I could see him dangling happiness before me like a bright, shiny diamond. Torn between my love for Reginald and love for my daughter, I inhaled a labored breath. The beating heart in my chest had been wounded time and again. I wanted Reginald, but I wanted to know of my daughter's welfare. Edward's eyes kept a steady stare on me as I contemplated my options.

"I'm weary," I replied glibly. "You offer your love, but I am in love with another man who I'm forbidden to see." Tears stung my eyes. "And now you tempt me with the singular promise of revealing my daughter's whereabouts. It's cruel."

"Love can be cruel," he replied coldly. "Nonetheless, Isabella, you must confess that when you gave yourself to a stable boy with no thought of consequences, you gave away more than your body. You relinquished your free choice in all aspects of your life, which changed its direction." He hesitated for a moment and then continued. "Is it a wonder that your father insists on making decisions for you after the poor choices of your past?"

His words pricked my heart. They were truthfully brutal. Nevertheless, I paid my price and matured as a result of it of that I was sure. I had evolved into a woman. Now a choice remained—what kind of woman would I be going forward? There were two options. A submissive girl or an independent female.

At that moment, the lights dimmed and my opportunity to escape to the powder room had vanished. Edward continued to hold my hand, rubbing his thumb across my flesh as if to soothe my sorrows. I turned and looked at him. Would it be so difficult to fall in love with another man? After all, he was titled, handsome, and wealthy, although I thought him rather of a serpent in character with a squeaky voice. The man knew what he wanted, which was more than I could say for myself. Did he possess the power to turn my heart from Reginald and give me the chance to see my daughter? I would never know unless I surrendered.

The remaining acts of the opera ensued, but like the first half, I found my mind wandering and not paying attention. As I heard the voice of the soprano reach the high notes, I relegated my struggle to an out-of-tune aria. There I was on stage. In the audience sat my parents. Reginald took a seat next to my mother while Edward sat next to my father. To be honest, I could never keep a tune, and I knew as soon as I opened my mouth they would laugh at my terrible pitch. Yes, my life had no harmony, and I needed to make a decision.

The performance ended, and Edward

held out his hand to help me from my seat. When I glanced in his eyes, he had returned to an attentive escort. An adoring smile curled the corner of his lips, and for some odd reason, I returned the gesture.

"We should catch a cab, or we will be late for our dinner reservations," he said, gesturing toward the exit.

"Of course." His hand slipped gently around my waist to guide me into the hallway, and afterward, he offered his arm. As we traversed the crowded hallway, I scanned the crowd, hoping to see Reginald. Naturally, I knew it would be highly unlikely to cross his path. Perhaps inwardly I wanted him to arrive as my knight in shining armor on a white horse to rescue me from this road I found myself walking. When we climbed into the cab, I pushed aside the foolish thought because no one would save me from the decision I needed to make.

After surviving the evening with Edward, I woke up the next morning with a slight headache, attributing the pain to too much champagne at dinner. The thought of hiding under my down-filled blanket the entire day felt tempting. Regrettably, in my alcohol stupor, I had agreed to another engagement with Edward. As I glanced at the clock, I moaned at the hour. He would arrive at nine o'clock to take me to West Sussex, two hours away. Another important horse competition, the Goodwood Glorious, was in its fourth day of events. This particular track, owned by the Duke of Richmond, had also garnished aristocratic popularity over the years. The affair wasn't as formal as the Royal Ascot, but I needed to dress appropriately and choose a hat. As I glanced at the window, I could see the sun seeping through the crack of the closed curtains. The English rain hadn't arrived to give me a reprieve.

A soft knock came at the door, and I heard Mother's voice.

"Isabella, are you awake?"

"Yes," I groaned. In an attempt to get out of bed, I swung my legs around and sat on the edge. Mother, rather than waiting for an invitation to enter, did so anyway. Her familiar sour facial expression beamed with anticipatory glee.

"Did you have a pleasant evening last night?"

"Somewhat," I answered, not giving her the satisfaction of bustling with delight over the affair.

"And today?"

"He is picking me up this morning to drive to West Sussex," I responded, twisting my lips in protest.

"Oh yes, he mentioned his plan to take you with him to the Goodwood races."

"I should think you would mind that he's spiriting me off out of town for a day trip." My motives were to incite worry in my mother regarding his behavior. Perhaps she would put a halt to the journey.

"No, not at all." She nonchalantly brushed off my comment. "There is a vast difference in character, Isabella, if you haven't noticed already, between stable trash and peers. Father and I trust him explicitly."

I don't, I thought to myself. A man is a man regardless if his trousers are from rags or riches. Nevertheless, I had already decided that if Edward did try anything, his nose would meet my clenched fist.

"If you would excuse me," I responded with a gloomy tone, "I need to get ready." I rose to my feet, avoiding eye contact.

"Well then, have a safe and enjoyable trip," she replied formally. Our seething animosity for one another chilled the air. As she retreated and closed the door behind her, I struggled to find an ounce of respect for the woman who had given me birth. We were vastly different from one another, and I amusingly wondered if I, too, had been adopted.

I pondered the day ahead as I bathed and dressed, attempting not to be late for the lord's arrival. My thoughts turned toward Reginald, reminding me that my heart remained wrapped in the agony of separation and despair. My yearning to be in his presence had not ceased, and I struggled with the situation that pulled me in the opposite direction.

After an hour of preparation, both physically and mentally, I descended the stairs to grab a quick bite to eat before Edward arrived. As I entered the dining room, to my surprise he sat at the table with my parents, drinking coffee and chatting. I halted at the threshold, cursing inwardly that my companion had already arrived. He lifted his head, and when he saw me, he rose to his feet.

"Good morning," he greeted with a sly smile.

"You're early," I replied, giving him no other comment in return. After I had retrieved a small portion of food, having lost my appetite, I sat down at the table across from him. My overt avoidance triggered my father to brandish me a disappointed look. He returned his attention to Edward.

"What horse are you betting on?"

"Well, I've missed the first few days," he complained. "It's the Chesterfield Cup today. I've had my eye on Irongrey, so I've placed a hefty bid on him to win."

"I lost a tidy sum at the Ascot," Father bemoaned. "If I give you a hundred pounds, will you put it on your favorite?"

"Absolutely," Edward replied. "To win?"

"Yes, to win."

Father handed him the money, and Edward slipped it into his pocket. It annoyed me how the two bantered between one another like old friends. Lord Ridley had weaseled his way into my family quickly, deepening relationships to his advantage.

The clock on the fireplace mantel chimed the nine o'clock hour. I pushed my plate away when I realized that my appetite had vanished after a few bites.

"We should be going," he said. He glanced at me and smiled warmly. "Are you ready?"

"Yes, let me get my hat and purse." Before I could push back my chair and rise, he had briskly moved behind me to help.

"Have a good day," my father said. He gave us both an approving look.

"When shall you be home?" My mother posed a surprising question.

"I should have your daughter back no later than ten o'clock this evening."

The entire day stretched before me like an eternity in purgatory. I ran upstairs to retrieve my things and returned a few minutes later to Edward waiting in the foyer.

"You look charming," he replied. "Nice bonnet."

"You look rather well-groomed yourself," I replied, surprised at the Panama sun hat he had donned. "No top hat?"

"Absolutely not at the Goodwood. Must keep up the fashion of Edward VII. He's the standard."

He flashed a toothy grin, wielding his charm, causing me to roll my eyes. Apparently, the man had planned to smother me today with his honey sweetness to gain my affection. My singular goal had been to resist him at all cost, but as we climbed into his car, I felt my resolve falter. The day would be long and challenging, of that I was sure.

Fifteen

Winners and Losers

Our two-hour drive proved tedious, to say the least. The chauffeur ignored us in the back seat. Naturally, I tried my best to keep conversation during the journey. Edward's personality dominated most topics, proving himself as snobbish and narrow-minded as I had earlier judged. Topics centered on his interests in life, ignoring my likes or dislikes. I felt like a hood ornament rather than a passenger in the car.

We pulled up to the estate and exited. A moment later, the driver drove off to park the vehicle somewhere on the vast landscape. Having never been to this particular event, my eyes scanned the scenery of rolling green hills. The air smelled of freshly cut grass sparkling in a brilliant green hue from the sun shining on each blade.

As we approached the stands, they

already brimmed with a huge crowd of men, women, jockeys, and horses. The fashions were less formal than at the Ascot. Nevertheless, the aristocratic members of society were recognizable by the chic styles in which they wore. I hadn't paid that much attention to my own but realized that I looked just as good as any other lady in attendance.

The atmosphere amongst the crowd bubbled with excitement. As I glanced at the faces of those nearby, not one of them frowned. They all appeared extremely cheerful and relaxed.

"I usually come for the entire four-day event and stay at the manor house," Edward noted. "Business held me back this year."

"Well, you are here now," I responded. "Are you a good judge of horses?" He smirked in arrogance as if my question were a foolish one to ask.

"Absolutely," he boasted. "Every good Englishman knows their horses."

The flamboyant statement did not surprise me. On the way here, he talked about his dream of owning a racehorse and traveling around England from event to event. As we wandered through the crowd, I could still hear his voice ringing in my ears about all his passionate outdoor pursuits that included golfing, hunting, and even motorcar racing. I concluded that his numerous leisurely activities took precedence over anything else in life. If he meant to impress me with his escapades, I frankly didn't care.

We walked amongst the crowd. Edward obtained a list of the upcoming races, which reminded me of my father's money still in his pocket. Rather than accuse him of forgetting about it on purpose, I gave him a gentle reminder. I inched over and cocked my head to see the race schedule.

"What horse will you be betting on for my father?" I asked nonchalantly.

"Bloody hell," he cursed. "I nearly forgot about it." He shoved his hand into his pocket and retrieved the hundred pounds. "I'll place it on Irongrey to win."

Mission accomplished; I smirked with satisfaction.

"Stay here, and I'll go place the wager."

"Here? Just stand here in the same spot while you're gone for who knows how long?" I protested. His suggestion gave no account for my well-being.

"Well then, why I don't walk you over to the refreshments. You can grab a table and wait there while I take care of it."

He grasped my hand and dragged me through the crowd rather crudely. An area had been set aside with tables, each having a large umbrella overhead for shade. We found an empty one, and he sat me down.

"Order whatever you like," he said.

After the quip, he turned and disappeared into the crowd, abandoning me. People mingled about, talking to one another, appearing carefree and happy. I, on the other hand, frowned as the misery of my situation became painfully evident. While my eyes scanned the attendees, they fell upon a couple, sipping drinks at a table a few yards away. I squinted my eyes in an attempt to focus. To my surprise, I saw Mr. and Mrs. Spencer from France.

Unable to stay seated any longer, I stood to my feet and walked directly toward their table with an eager spring in my step.

"Catherine!" I called her name a few feet away, and she turned her head in the direction of my voice.

"Isabella? Is that you?" She rose to her feet as did her husband. Their warm smiles flooded my heart with joy.

"Oh, it is so good to see you," I blubbered. My arms wrapped around her tightly, giving Catherine a hug.

"My goodness," she replied. "How well you look." She turned toward Mr. Spencer. "Doesn't she look beautiful?"

"Indeed," he grinned.

"What are you doing here?" I inquired excitedly.

"For the races, of course. The Glorious is one of our favorites," she replied. "We do occasionally return to England on holiday, you know, to visit Reginald."

"Are you staying with him?" The thought of Reginald being nearby caused my eyes to glance through the crowd.

"Yes, but he's not here," she replied.

"Oh." My voice dropped in a disappointed tone.

"You're not alone here, are you?" Catherine asked with a worried look on her face.

"No, I'm not. I do have an escort," I

replied, not wishing to elaborate. "He's placing a wager for my father."

"Well, why don't you sit down and join us?" Mr. Spencer offered. It will probably take him a while. He pulled out a chair for me, which I readily accepted. It felt wonderful to be in their presence, reminding me how much I missed good company. My life had become an isolated and orchestrated affair, denying me the simple pleasures of pleasant companionship.

"How long will you be in England?" My curiosity might have been somewhat prying, but I hoped to see them more than once.

"We leave in a few days," Mr. Spencer replied. "We've been here almost two weeks."

"Two weeks?" I replied. It bothered me that Reginald hadn't told me of their arrival. Of course, he had no reason to let me know.

"Do you think that you'll be moving back to England?" I asked. "Reginald spoke of his concern that you should return."

Catherine and her husband exchanged glances. "Yes, he continues to pressure us to do so, and we have seriously thought about returning." Her smile faded. "We do have concerns regarding the political situation in nearby countries."

"It would be wonderful if you could," I enthusiastically added. "I count you both as dear friends."

"How very kind," Catherine replied.

I couldn't help but wonder if Reginald had mentioned our short, budding romance. Perhaps I should have left it as an unapproachable subject, but I could not.

"Your son was most kind in escorting me back home when I left. Did he tell you that we met on the train?"

Mr. Spencer cleared his throat. "Yes, he mentioned it. He also stated that he found you to be a delightful young lady."

"When he told me that his wife had passed away, my heart ached for him. Such tragedy not only for him but for their child." The thought still brought grief to my heart as I broached the subject.

Catherine glanced at her husband again as if they both needed to formulate a proper response. Finally she spoke.

"Her passing was a great loss to

everyone and a shock."

They both appeared to fall into a digestive silence for a few minutes, which gave me concern. A part of me wanted to tell them of my love for Reginald, but I feared the consequences and kept silent.

"I respect your son very much," I finally confessed. "He is a kind and attentive man."

"He speaks affectionately of you," Catherine answered. Her eyes sparkled as if she approved of our mutual regard for one another.

At that moment, I thought perhaps the door had opened to express my true feelings. The words, on the tip of my tongue, were ready to declare. However, the moment quickly vanished with the return of Edward.

"There you are." He scowled at me. "I've been looking for you for ten minutes. You should have stayed at the table where I left you."

Embarrassed that he scolded me in front of my friends, I felt my cheeks blush. "Edward, these are dear friends of mine." My eyes narrowed at him to behave. "Mrs. and Mrs. Spencer, this is Lord Ridley, my escort."

Escort. It would be the only term I would give the man. I would not call him my beau or my future fiancé or whatever other title of importance he wanted me to give.

"Pleased to meet you," Mr. Spencer replied. He reached out and shook Edward's hand.

"Pleasure," Catherine said. She glanced at me with empathy in her eyes. "Isabella is quite right. We are old friends and just happened to bump into each other. Forgive us for pulling her away."

If anyone should apologize, it should have been Edward for his snippy arrival. As I looked into his eyes, the realization of who the couple happened to be apparently dawned on him at that moment. His countenance turned dark.

"Are you ready?" he said, looking at me with a displeased glare. "The race is about to start, and I'd like to get a good view."

I turned toward the Spencers and smiled graciously. "Seeing you today has been the highlight of my existence." Unable to walk away, I stepped forward and hugged

Catherine again. "I love you like a mother," I whispered in her ear.

"And I you like a daughter," she replied in secret. "Don't despair, my dearest. All will turn out as it should."

Her words brought comfort to my heart even though I wondered what she meant by them. We released each other, and I glanced at Mr. Spencer.

"Good-bye."

"Isabella." He nodded. "Do take care of yourself." His fatherly tone revealed concern in his voice.

"I will."

Edward, naturally impatient, grabbed my hand and tugged me away from their presence.

"The race is about to start," he reiterated.

After finding a viewing spot that suited him, he quickly engrossed himself in the competition. The pounding hooves of the horses passed by, making their way around the course. Perhaps I should have shown more interest, but I felt nothing. Instead, my eyes glanced through the crowd, attempting to see the Spencers, but they were nowhere in sight. I should have told Catherine, I inwardly scolded myself for the missed opportunity. If I had confessed my love for her son, maybe she would have talked some sense into Reginald to keep pursuing me regardless of my father's objections.

Edward's yelling drew my attention back to the race. The crowd turned into the usual frenzy of excitement as the horses approached the finish line.

"Come on," he bellowed.

Since I didn't even know what number Irongrey wore, I couldn't tell if he was ahead or behind. As they crossed into victory or loss, Edward appeared ecstatic over the results.

"What a race," he shouted. "Did you see that?"

Of course, I didn't know what I saw but nodded my head in agreement. "He won, I take it."

"Yes, he won."

He looked at me and smirked. Before I could protest, he had pulled me into his arms and kissed me. My eyes grew wide rather than shutting them at the onslaught. Over his shoulder, I caught Mr. and Mrs.

Spencer watching the two of us. Not wanting them to tell Reginald the scene, I swiftly pushed away Edward.

"Do you always kiss a woman without asking first?"

"Why shouldn't I kiss my prize?" he dryly said. "You think the Spencers will go back and tell your Reginald we're in love? Is that what you're worried about?"

His sharp response irked me. As if he wanted them to see his next move, his hand brushed across my cheek in a possessive manner.

"You might as well forget it, Isabella. The man cannot and will not cross your father. He has too much to lose." He slipped his arm around my waist and pulled me to his side. "Besides, I have something you want, don't I?"

My daughter. Yes, he did have something that I desperately wanted, for which I would probably end up selling my soul.

"Now, why don't we try that again," he seductively slurred, "before I collect your father's winnings and mine."

Edward pulled me toward him and

lowered his lips upon mine. This time he kissed me without the grand fervency of the last. Instead, he wielded his manly charms, attempting to woo me as a female. My mind screamed "resist him" the entire time. Instead, my body had something else to say about the matter. Unable to control my womanly needs, I pulled away in frustration.

"You've made your point," I said, warily looking at him. By the arrogant look in his eye, he knew that he had just touched a weakness—my flesh.

"Do you want to come with me?"

My eyes darted around, but the Spencers had disappeared again into the crowd. "All right," I acquiesced. "I'm sure my father will be thrilled with the win."

"Yes, there are winners and losers in all aspects of life," he sardonically replied.

His reference had nothing to do with horses and everything to do with Reginald.

SIXTEEN

MERRY-GO-ROUND

The weeks passed one by one with no word from Reginald. Unable to keep quiet, I wrote him a letter, posting it to his office. In bold letters I penned the word "confidential" on the envelope, hoping it would be delivered but remain unopened. The words were short and to the point. "I need to see you on a matter of urgent business." Whether he refused to answer, or the office staff had confiscated the letter, I had no idea. His silence left me with little choice than to continue Edward's attempt to court me in the hopes of marriage.

My parents had no qualms about inviting him to dine with us as often as possible. On the other evenings, he took me to dinner to lavish restaurants, the opera, and theater shows. The seasonal horse racing continued through September and October, and I accompanied him as his female companion. During the outings, I met more of his social circle but found no new friendships among the women or men.

When Reginald failed to answer, I found the grief of our failing relationship difficult to handle. In spite of his silence, my love for him remained steady. Irrationally I continued to hope something would change.

As far as Edward was concerned, my tolerance for him grew at the same time. At least he kept me occupied and busy. Otherwise, I would have continued to pine away over Reginald. The only thing that kept me following the snake down the path had been the knowledge regarding my daughter's whereabouts.

My mother and father often asked if he had proposed yet, but Edward had not. I had no doubt, nevertheless, that he believed I belonged to him already. His confessions of love were heartfelt and his behavior gentlemanly. Though his kisses passionately enticed my female hormones, he kept his distance and did not pressure me for sexual favors.

Something in me felt as if I were

traveling on a merry-go-round about to make another foolish mistake in my life. I had finally resigned myself that no other options existed. My happiness in the arms of Reginald would not occur, and as a result, I finally surrendered, if you will, to the inevitable. If Edward proposed, I would accept. At least I would be well cared for and loved. To add to the enticement, I would finally be able to leave home.

Did I love him? He would never capture my soul like Reginald. Perhaps one day I would affectionately tolerate him because he held the key to the whereabouts and welfare of my daughter. If I ever had the opportunity to see her, I would seize it at a moment's notice.

As he returned me one evening to my home, he must have sensed my change in heart. He had become overly attentive and sweet our entire time together. When he walked me to the door, I was about to invite him in for an evening drink, but he halted and made a comment.

"You're different this evening."

He warmly smiled at me and slipped his arm around my waist. When he drew me close to his body, I tilted my head back and looked into his eyes.

"You once told me to surrender," I replied.

"I did." His fingers brushed a drooping curl near my eye. "And have you?"

"Perhaps."

"Well now." He breathed. "If that's the case, then it might be an opportune time to propose."

"Then propose," I flatly replied with no emotion. Perhaps I expected him to go down on one knee, but he didn't. He merely pulled me toward his body and hotly whispered in my ear.

"Marry me, Isabella."

I could have instantly replied yes, but I did not. He wanted me, and I wanted something from him. We were about to strike a bargain—not a marriage.

"If you assure me that you will keep your promise and tell me about my daughter's whereabouts." I wrapped my arms around his neck and stared into his eyes. "Then yes, I will marry you."

"You are so determined," he slyly drawled, narrowing his eyes. "Yes, I will keep my promise."

Frankly, I don't know why I initiated the next move. Maybe my actions came from gratefulness, but I knew they didn't come from love. My lips met his, and I kissed him, yielding my life and future for the sake of a secret. Edward, enjoying my forward and uninhibited response, pushed me up against the stone pillar by the doorway. His hardened manhood pressed against my pelvis, and I knew that he wanted me. I wasn't about to give him my body yet.

When I pulled away from him, he stepped back and flashed a wicked grin. "I've been carrying this in my pocket for a few weeks, waiting for the right time." He slipped his hand into his trousers and pulled out a diamond ring.

"Just waiting for the right time?" I snickered.

"Surrender is better than battle," he quipped. "Your affection is important to me."

"Well, here is my hand." I held it out and waited. Edward slipped a gaudy diamond up my finger, which frankly I thought hideous in style.

"Thank you." I turned my hand right and left trying to find something endearing about the jewel of our engagement. "I suppose you should ask my father."

"Already done," he said, posturing himself before me. "I did so weeks ago, and he readily accepted me as his future son-in-law."

"Did he now," I replied. "And did my mother also give you the seal of approval?"

"A kiss of support on my cheek," he boasted.

"Aren't you lucky," my voice drawled sarcastically. I knew they both would be ecstatic to get me out of the residence and married off. Well, their plotting and manipulation had paid off.

As far as Edward's parents were concerned, they were dead, so he had no immediate family to make my acquaintance. My mind drifted toward Catherine and Mr. Spencer, thinking about how I would have loved to have them as my in-laws. It would have been a perfect union with Reginald. As a stepmother to his child, I could have found purpose, bore him additional children, and actually spend the remainder of my days with the man I adored. Edward had merely been my consolation for love lost and purgatory for my foolish mistake of years ago.

Yes, I had climbed upon the merry-go-round for another spin, making an equally impetuous decision. Perhaps that was my destiny in life—to repeat my mistakes.

The next morning, I arrived at the breakfast table to announce our engagement. Father sat doing his usual morning routine of reading the mail, which only reminded me of my unanswered letter to Reginald. Mother sipped her tea, staring at the wall as if she had no purpose in life. Sadly, I knew that to be true.

After sitting down with my plate, I broke the silence. A lump had formed in my throat because I hated to admit, even to them, that I had surrendered to their will. After clearing my airway with a few short coughs, I opened my mouth and held up my hand.

"Edward proposed last evening, and I accepted."

Mother's head turned in my direction

and broke out in a smile. "You did?"

"It's what you wanted, isn't it?"

"Well, congratulations are definitely in order," Father added.

"Edward mentioned that he already spoke with you about the matter." Naturally, I wanted to confirm that to be true though I had no reason to doubt.

"Absolutely. The young man did approach me for your hand in marriage, and I heartily approved."

As if a demon had caught the tip of my tongue, I couldn't help but snidely remark my real feelings. "Yes, I'm sure you did approve. Thankfully, it wasn't Reginald Spencer on his knee, or you would have had him thrown out of the house." My fork stabbed my scrambled eggs, and I jammed them into my mouth to silence myself further. God forbid, I should speak with my mouth full.

"I don't know what you're complaining about," Mother interjected. "Edward Ridley is a far better match on all accounts."

I swallowed hard, pushing the eggs down my throat. "Father, I'll need your generous wallet for a wedding dress. I want all the frills and thrills of a beautiful wedding since this is your matchmaking dream."

"Don't you love the man?" He looked at me cockeyed.

"I tolerate him because he has something that I want." Naturally, I wasn't about to tell them what that something happened to be.

"There is no question in my mind that he loves you, Isabella." My mother attempted to reason with me that his romantic feelings should satisfy me, regardless.

"I have no doubt of it."

"Then you may have as your heart desires. I will let you and your mother plan the affair. Have you set a date?"

"Yes, we spoke of mid-November."

"Oh my, that's barely enough time," Mother groaned. "So soon?"

"I think it is best that our nuptials occur sooner than later because I doubt you would like me to have the time to reconsider my decision."

"November it is then," Father heartily agreed.

"Good." Another forkful of eggs filled my mouth. What should have been a happy announcement had turned me into a sour mood. *Keep thinking of Mary Jane, and you will be fine.* It would be my new mantra for the weeks ahead to keep me focused until my vows.

Keep thinking of Mary Jane.

SEVENTEEN

I WILL – I WON'T

They were the two most difficult words I had ever uttered in my entire life.

"I will."

Edward's face glowed in conquest as he watched me confess my acceptance of him as a husband. He had triumphed and gotten his way. In fact, as I stood there I realized everyone had gotten their way—Edward, Mother, Father, and even Reginald. I, on the other hand, had failed miserably.

The remaining ceremony passed before me in a daze. When it ended, I turned toward the man who owned my soul, awaiting the sealing kiss. Edward did not hesitate to scoop me in his arms and declare his victory in front of the congregation. He nearly knocked me off-balance, and I stumbled. The congregation apparently enjoyed the scene as they laughed at my predicament.

"May I present to you Mr. and Mrs. Edward and Isabella Ridley," the vicar announced.

We turned and faced the congregation, making our way down the aisle to the vestibule, passing the smiling congratulatory claps. Soon guests would shower us in rice in honor of my hopeful forthcoming fertility.

We halted our step at the doorway, and I turned to Edward and asked for the last time.

"I have kept my promise and married you," I asserted calmly. "Now keep yours. Where is my daughter?" A sardonic smile curled the corner of his mouth.

"Well, now that you are my wife, I suppose it doesn't matter if I tell you today or later." He paused for a moment and smirked. "There is nothing you can do about it."

"Well?" I pressured him again.

"Reginald and Catrina Spencer adopted your daughter," he announced. "Of course, the poor man lost his wife, which your father hadn't counted upon."

My chest constricted as if the boa snake

had taken it and crushed it in a death-gripping squeeze. I could not breathe. Blotches of black danced before my vision as if I would faint at any moment. As I stood gasping for air, the congregation had begun to make their way toward us, pressing us out the door toward the shower of rice. The wicked man, who I now called my husband, mockingly laughed at my reaction. At that moment, I lost all composure, and months of pent-up unacted-upon anger spewed forth like a volcano.

"You bloody serpent," I railed at the top of my voice. Without a second thought, I took my bouquet and shoved it in Edward's smirking face, grinding the roses into his nose, eyes, and cheeks. The crushed petals fell on his fancy suit, and he grabbed my hand in protest.

"What the hell?" he mumbled underneath the flowers.

I released the bouquet, pulled my hand away from his, and the destroyed flowers fell at his feet. Rather than fight, I fled, so I raised my skirt and sprinted down the pathway from the church door toward the street. My veil flew into the air above my head while my long train dragged across the walkway. As I did so, I could hear my parents' voices frantically calling my name, mingled with Edward's wailing voice.

Seeing an approaching cab, I hysterically hailed it with my arms flailing above my head. He stopped, I flung open the door, and climbed inside.

"Go, go," I shouted, turning around to see Edward almost grabbing the door handle as the cab drove away. The surprised cabby turned his head around and snickered.

"Where to, ma'am?"

"To 160 Regent Street," I replied. "And hurry, please."

"Will do," he amusingly replied, stepping on the gas pedal.

I swung my head around and peered out the back window glad to see that I had left them all behind. The driver glanced at me in the rearview mirror, chuckling at my antics and apparent urgency in fleeing the church. He probably thought that I had changed my mind at the altar, and I wished to God I had.

It then dawned on me that I had no

money to pay the fare. I glanced down at the wedding ring on my finger and slid it off.

"I'm afraid I have nothing to pay you with," I sheepishly admitted. "But I do have this ring." I held it out to him. "Would this be sufficient to pay the fare?"

He glanced at me, and his eyes widened. "Let me see," he said, holding out his hand.

I placed the ring in his palm, and he examined it while driving. At first I thought he would run the cab off the road as he weaved in the lane, gawking at the stone.

"Are you sure?"

"Yes, I'm sure."

"That's worth a pretty penny," he said, grinning. "More than the fare you will owe me when we get there, that's for sure."

"Take it," I implored. "I hate it anyway, and you've just rescued me."

We pulled up to the office of Reginald's firm, and I opened the door. "Is it a deal? The ring for my fare?"

"If you're sure," he said. "Would be a nice present for my wife."

"Well, I hope she enjoys it." I slammed the cab door shut. "Thank you." He drove off, and I pulled up my skirt and headed for the entrance. People on the sidewalk gawked at me as if I were crazy, but I didn't care. With my train dragging behind me, I sprinted up the stairs and burst through the double doors. Finding myself in a reception area, I approached the desk. The girl behind it jumped to her feet in surprise, eying my dress up and down with envy in her eyes.

"May I help you?"

"Reginald Spencer," I demanded. "I want to see him. Where is his office?"

Rather than arguing with me, she flashed a silly grin and pointed toward a door down the hallway.

"First door on your right."

Sick of the veil dragging down my back, I pulled out the tiara that held it in place and handed it over to the young lady.

"Here take it," I said, shoving it in her direction. "You might want to use it someday." A second later, I strode toward the door. Reginald didn't deserve a polite knock. Instead, I turned the doorknob, shoved open the barrier, and dashed inside. I expected him to be sitting at his desk, but he stood by the window, staring out into the street. When he heard me, he swung around. The shock of my arrival drained the color from his face.

"Isabella, what are you doing here?" He eyed me up and down in my wedding gown.

"How could you?" I screamed in response, balling my fists at my side.

"How could I do what?" Confused by my challenging question, he scowled in defense.

Angry and shaking, I took a step in his direction, fully intending to spew every malicious thought swirling around my head.

"Allow me to marry Edward Ridley when all along you had my daughter in your care." My voice trembled. "You knew I loved you," I cried. "What a despicable and cruel thing to do to me."

Reginald's eyes, downcast and sad, displayed distress. "I couldn't tell you," he coolly answered. "Your father forbade it. I signed a legal document of confidentiality."

"Who cares if my father forbade it?"

"Believe me, there were plenty of times I wanted to tell you, Isabella. Truly, I did," he urgently assured me.

"Well, Edward knew and used it as leverage to get me to marry him. He promised to tell me the whereabouts of my daughter once we married, and he just did."

"You married him?"

"Yes, I married him, and I just left him after shoving my bouquet in his face." I thought about the satisfaction it brought me, easing my misery. "Look at me," I implored, lifting my arms up at my side. "Why else would I be standing here in a wedding dress?"

Reginald paused for a few moments, considering my state, and with an unsteady voice asked, "You love him though, don't you?"

How could he be so daft? I eyed him in disbelief at his foolish assumption. "No, I love you," I cried. "Did I not repeatedly tell you of my affections and wishes?"

"Isabella," he groaned. "I'm so, so sorry."

"Sorry? That's all you can say?" My brokenhearted cry apparently made no difference.

"It's too late now. You are married, and I've made plans to leave England."

Astonished at his admission, I stepped closer. "Leave England?" As soon as my question left my lips, Father and Edward barged into the office.

"I told you she'd be here," my father crowed.

Edward, seething in rage, demanded my obedience.

"Come with me," he barked like a rabid dog, holding out his hand.

"I'm going nowhere," I replied, gritting my teeth. My entire body trembled in wrath. "You both disgust me." My ladylike demeanor disappeared. The time had arrived to give everyone a piece of my mind. "You," I screamed, taking an angry step in my father's direction, "have orchestrated and perpetrated a wicked deception." I eyed him up and down. "You call yourself an upstanding man of character, and I can barely look at you."

"Don't you talk to me in that fashion, young lady," he shrilled. My father's nostrils flared as he rebuked me like a child.

"It's about time I talked to you in that fashion and stood up for myself," I countered in frustration. "I am a grown woman and not some sixteen-year-old foolish girl any longer." He fell silent, which turned my attention toward Edward.

"As for you, I'll be damned if you think I am going to consummate this marriage with a conniving serpent like you. You have emotionally blackmailed me since the moment we met." I wanted to spit in his face. "I demand an annulment."

"You can't do that to me," Edward protested indignantly. "Who in the hell do you think you are, giving me orders? You're my wife only a few minutes ago vowing obedience."

His idiotic response caused me to burst out in laughter. I turned toward Reginald. "Tell me, solicitor, can I get an annulment?"

"You probably have grounds on fraud and coercion," he responded. A glint of hope brightened Reginald's eyes, but I wasn't done with him either. Unfortunately, he too would receive a piece of my mind. Trying to control my anger, I made my own demands.

"I want my daughter back, Reginald."

"You can't have that girl back," my father interjected. "You signed her away."

"No, you signed her away to keep the scandal from the family name," I protested. "You didn't ask me—you told me."

"You are damn right I did." His chest heaved up and down in anger. "You brought shame to the family, and I had to clean up your mess."

My mess—my mistake—my fault. I wanted to scream at the top of my lungs. "What breaks my heart, even more, is that you have denied your own flesh and blood. My daughter is an innocent child in all this, and you have treated her like a pawn in a chess game." His cold stare radiated denial, confirming his heartless condition like that of my mother's. "Have you even seen her?"

"I don't care to see her," he replied. "Sired by a stable boy, she has no part in our family name or inheritance."

His words thrust through my heart like a knife. I needed to protect my baby, and as her mother, I would. My gaze turned back toward Reginald, hoping that he would speak up in my defense and be the man I wanted him to be. By then, his associate had entered the office to see what the ruckus was about.

"What's going on?"

I answered before giving anyone else a chance. "I'm fixing the mess these three men have made of my life." He looked at me in my attire and glanced at everyone with a befuddled expression on his face. "You're welcome to stay and watch," I added, "but stay out of it."

Again, I turned and looked at Reginald. "I want my daughter returned to me. It's my duty to raise her not yours." The tone of my voice calmed somewhat as I entreated the man I loved to do the right thing. All I knew at that moment was that I wanted my baby back in my arms regardless of the sacrifices I would need to make to care for her.

"Don't you dare give her that little girl," my father growled at Reginald with a threatening glare.

"Reginald?" I looked at him, waiting for him to do or say something, but he looked indecisive, which irritated me to no end.

"You will get no support from me," my father snapped, "if you intend on taking that child."

"And you'll get nothing from me either if you annul this marriage." Edward threw his threat into the circle. Neither of them frightened me. Once again, I glanced at Reginald. Our eyes met, and I witnessed a change in his demeanor. He pulled his shoulders back and stood tall. After glancing at my father and Edward with as much disgust as I held, he spoke directly to me in a tender voice.

"Marry me, Isabella," he calmly asked. "Be my wife and be the mother you always wanted to be to your little girl."

"She can't marry you. She's married to me!" Edward howled. Reginald ignored his ranting.

Suddenly his boss decided to enter the ring of fire with his opinion. "If you marry that woman, you're fired!"

Reginald glanced at everyone, shook his head, and chuckled. "Don't bother," he said. "I quit. I had planned on giving my notice today, regardless."

"Quit? What do you mean you quit?"

"I received an offer of employment yesterday from a firm in New York, which I accepted."

New York? Reginald had planned on leaving. They could have disappeared from my life for eternity had I not lost my senses and ran here to confront him. Inwardly I panicked.

"Why?" I gulped.

"Your father suggested for everyone's sake that I leave the country with your daughter and never return. Now I wish to thank him for it." Reginald approached and stood in front of me.

"I love you," he said, reaching out and taking my hand. "I have loved you all along." He kissed it softly, rekindling the affection we had buried. "I want to marry you, my darling Isabella."

"Get me an annulment, and I'll marry you," I replied without hesitation. My heart swelled at the thought of being his wife. I could see Edward and my father out of the corner of my eye, gaping at the scene in protest.

"Come with me, and I'll introduce you to your daughter." Reginald took my hand and led me toward the office door.

"Where in the hell do you think you're going?" Edward balked.

I halted in my steps, turned around, and looked at him. "I'm going to meet my baby and then make love to Reginald instead of to you." I flashed a mocking grin. "Do think of me while you are lying in bed alone tonight. I will not be thinking of you."

"Then give me the ring back," he snarled.

"Oh, the ring? I'm sorry." I giggled unashamedly. "I used it to pay the cabby for my fare here." I held up my left hand, wiggling my bare finger in front of him.

"You bloody gave it away? Do you know how much that diamond was worth?" Edward's chest heaved up and down.

"I thought it hideously ugly," I added.

My eyes shifted toward my father, who looked as if he were on the verge of a heart attack. I had no parting words to give him. He had lost a daughter and granddaughter. As far as my parents were concerned, I held no affection for either.

"Let's go, Reginald." He smiled warmly at me, put his arm around my waist, and led me outdoors. As we passed the receptionist, she called to me.

"Do you want your veil back?"

"No, keep it," I said, not wanting to remember that I had just gotten married. I was sure she would enjoy the diamond tiara to which it was attached.

By the time we reached the sidewalk,

my body shivered from head to foot. We stopped by the curb to hail a cab, but Reginald took me in his arms to kiss me first. As soon as our lips met, I knew that finally I had gotten what I wanted

EIGHTEEN

SUGAR AND SPICE

As we sat side by side in the backseat of the cab, my emotions of the past few hours overcame my dry eyes. I felt a tear trickle down my cheek at the expectation of what lay ahead. In a few minutes I would see my daughter. As I pondered the meeting, I suddenly felt concerned.

"I don't think that you should introduce me to her as her mother," I announced. "It will confuse her, I'm sure."

"I think that's wise," Reginald announced. "I shall tell her that you are daddy's special friend."

"Look at me though." I laughed. "I'm in a wedding dress. It's not exactly the most appropriate attire to be meeting a toddler."

"You do look stunning, by the way," he added with a twinkle in his eye. "Mother left a few items of clothing from her last visit. You can change into one of her things."

"Will you actually move to New York? What about your parents?" I dreaded the thought of them remaining in France.

"I'm happy to say that they have decided to return to England. They will be living in my home while I'm away." His smile faded, and he looked at me with concern. "You will come with me, won't you?"

"Of course," I assured him. "Will I be able to get an annulment?"

"Don't worry about that now, Isabella. I'll take care of it."

The cab slowed and pulled up to a Georgian-style house in a quaint area of the city. After it had stopped, Reginald paid the fare and helped me out. The prospect of seeing my little girl sent a shiver of excitement through my body. Reginald reached out, took my hand, and squeezed it tight.

"She's probably taking her afternoon nap, so you have an opportunity to slip upstairs and change."

"All right," I said, following him. We entered into his home, and a stout woman greeted our arrival.

"Mr. Spencer," she said, glancing at my attire and at him. "You are home early."

"Quite so," Reginald replied. "Is Mary asleep?"

"Mary?" I repeated. "Did you name her Mary?"

Reginald smiled. "Mother told me she heard you whisper Mary Jane, so Catrina and I agreed to have her baptized as such."

"Oh, Reginald," I cried. My hand came to my mouth, stifling a grateful cry.

"Yes, sir, she's asleep but should be waking soon."

"Very well." Reginald took my hand and led me upstairs. "Come with me, sweetheart."

As we ascended the stairs, I struggled with all the unanswered questions that haunted me since I gave birth.

"Why?" I asked. "Why did you and Catrina adopt her?"

We arrived at the landing of the second floor, and Reginald halted his step. "Catrina could not have children. We had tried for some time."

"How sad," I replied.

"Your father had been aware that we

were considering adoption. He approached the two of us and offered your baby, with conditions of course."

"Conditions?"

"You were never to know," he acknowledged.

Reginald directed me to a guest room, opened a closet, and found a dress for me to wear. "Here, I'm sure Mother won't mind. Go ahead and change, and I'll be back in a few minutes."

I nodded in agreement, and Reginald departed, closing the door behind him. It did not take long to rid myself of the wedding dress. The ceremony had been beautiful, and Father had given me everything I asked for in return for marrying Edward. The thought that I had done so sickened me, but I had gained the truth because of it. Perhaps I hadn't made a mistake after all. It had become a means to an end.

As I finished putting on the dress, a soft knock came at the door. "Come in."

A moment later, Reginald entered, but he was not alone. In his arms, rubbing her sleepy eyes, sat a little girl. The shock of finally seeing my baby after having given birth sent my soul soaring toward the heavens. I stood speechless, looking at her form. She had golden tresses that twirled in ringlets to her shoulders. Beautiful blue eyes gazed at me curiously.

"Can you say hello, Mary Jane?" Reginald prompted her with a smile. "This lovely lady has come to visit you."

My daughter suddenly became shy and buried her head in Reginald's shoulder. "It's all right, sweetheart," he assured her. "She is a very nice lady."

"Hello, Mary Jane." My voice trembled. I took a step closer, trying not to frighten her with my approach. "Did you have a good nap?" She peeked at me and then shook her head yes.

"She can be a little timid, but give her time and she'll come around."

"Oh, Reginald, she is beautiful." I couldn't take my eyes off her, and I desperately wanted to touch her. "Do you think she'll let me hold her?"

"She might," he answered. "Mary Jane, would you like to say hello to my friend?"

I held out my arms toward her and

smiled. She stared at me guardedly for a few moments, and Reginald stepped closer.

"Can I hold you?" She glanced at Reginald and then held out her arms to me. A smile burst across my face, and in the next moment, a little girl of sugar and spice clung to me.

"She's back where she belongs," Reginald said.

"We are all where we belong." Mary Jane giggled at the two of us, and I remembered Catherine's words.

"Don't despair, my dearest. All will turn out as it should."

~The End~

ABOUT THE AUTHOR

With Russian blood on my father's side and English on my mother's, I blame my ancestors for the lethal combination of my DNA that influences my stories. Tragedy and drama might be found between the pages, but I eventually give readers a happy ending.

I live in the beautiful, but rainy, Pacific Northwest. My hobby (more of an obsession) is researching my English ancestry and expanding my family tree. To keep the memory of my ancestors alive, I often use their names in my novels.

My usual genre is historical fiction with romantic elements and historical romance set in the Victorian and Edwardian eras. My books include:

- ❖ The Price of Innocence (Permanently Free) – Book One of the Legacy Series
- ❖ The Price of Deception – Book Two of the Legacy Series

- ❖ The Price of Love – Book Three of the Legacy Series
- ❖ The Price of Passion – Book Four of the Legacy Series
- ❖ The Legacy Series Box Set (Books 1-4)
- ❖ The Phantom of Valletta (Featured in The Sunday Times, Malta in 2010)
- ❖ Dark Persuasion (2012 Finalist in the USA Best Book Awards for Romance)
- ❖ A Portrait of Perfection (A Dark Gothic Tale of Love and Betrayal)
- ❖ A Christmas Oath (2015 Christmas Novelette)
- ❖ A Christmas Mission (2016 Christmas Novelette)
- ❖ Lady Isabella (Ladies of Disgrace)

Romance With a Kiss of Suspense, under the pen name of Nora Covington. Works to date include:

- ❖ Thorncroft Manor
- ❖ Whitefield Hall
- ❖ Blythe Court – Five-Star Readers' Favorite Review
- ❖ Romance With a Kiss of Suspense Box Set

Contemporary Romance:

 ❖ Conflicting Hearts, by J.D. Burrows,
   Five-Star Reader's Favorite Review -
   Contemporary romance/women's
   fiction.

Sign Up for my Newsletter and Author
Blog by visiting my Official Website

http://vickihopkins.com